Silence Of The Grid

By Bill Gear

In the absence of light, there is darkness. Darkness will rule when the machines are unleashed. When AI becomes God. God cares no more. All that is left is death and destruction!

In the coming years, Artificial Intelligence systems will become mainstream. People will stop making decisions and the machines will act on their own. We will think we are in control, but we will not be. We will think we are safe but won't. The inventions of humans will outpace their own intelligence. This story depicts a group of zealots who use AI to forward their ideology. Like Pandora's box, once it is open, it can't be closed.

From the Author

Thank you all for purchasing the first book in my new series. The story and the characters took months to create. You may notice some of my characters are carried over from book to book. My characters represent people I have met or known over my entire life. I always say real life is stranger than fiction, so my stories start from my life experiences, dreams, and nightmares. I am still not a professional writer; this is just my hobby. Come join it with me.

This is the start of the Silence of the Grid series. Since I work in the IT field and am a hard-core prepper, this book seemed easy to write. I took a lot of liberties with the technology I described to make it more interesting. IT is boring by nature, so I tried to jazz it up a bit. More books will come as my demented little mind thinks them up. I hope you will join Blake and Lorain on their apocalyptic holiday as they experience the downfall and rebirth of humanity through this series.

Future titles in the series:

From the Ashes - A "Silence of the Grid" story
Someone from the Stormm's past has survived, their harrowing story of survival make Blake and Lorain's seem like child's play.

Blake and Lorain - A "Silence of the Grid" prequel
Blake and Lorain meet in the most romantic place ever, work. Follow the two as they meet, fall in love, and find themselves being stalked by a former Marine Scout Sniper with only one goal: to kill Blake and steal Lorain. Blake must act; his family and future cannot wait for the police.

A Seven Year Stormm - A "Silence of the Grid" prequel
Blake Stormm is not the mild-mannered IT guy he portrays. He has a seedy hidden past that not even his beloved Lorain knows about. Follow Blake as he rages through a seven-year part of his questionable past.

Crashing Moon - A "Silence of the Grid" follow up
One hundred years in the future. The planet has recovered. The lines have been redrawn; new countries and leaders battle for dominance. The distant Stormm descendants are still in the game. Not known to anyone, the super AI virus crashed a research vehicle into an unsuspecting asteroid a hundred years ago. That act will bring the Earth to its final days.

Contents

Prologue.

Blake Stormm was an IT security analyst at a local community college. After 25 years in the business, Blake possessed a unique understanding of the digital world that few could rival. His research revealed a chilling prophecy: a cyber-attack of unprecedented scale was looming, one that threatened to dismantle the world as he knew it. Blake spoke of secret communications, machines talking to machines, and patterns of vulnerabilities unlike any before.

As an old school IT guy, Blake had always wanted to know how everything worked. He would teach his underlings how to start at the root of the problem. Too many hours were always wasted chasing the symptoms instead of solving the problem. Over the years Blake has written or acquired a mass of utilities, programs, and scripts to navigate his daily work. Almost kicking and screaming, Blake was being pulled from his old school ways into the artificial intelligence world.

Blake was finally dragged into the AI world by his boss signing a five-year contract with the Morison Algorithm Alliance, a Silicon Valley Artificial Intelligence startup. This gave him access to 17 forms of Artificial Intelligence for his daily work for everything from coding, traffic monitoring, to analyzing security logs. He would be uploading massive amounts of data to these supposedly secure AI environments every day.

The responses from these did not impress Blake. He swore sometimes that these were programmed by spoiled little children. These self-learning algorithm engines were supposedly custom-built for their tasks and sometimes returned valuable insight. But more often than not, he would have to double check or manually calculate out the answers himself. All the recent vulnerability patches coming out, compounded with these AI services spitting out garbage, could not just be a coincidence, something was happening.

Blake would soon sound the alarm, but his warnings would be met with skepticism by his peers and the college's general administration. Even though Blake had been preparing for something like this for 30 years, what would he do? Would he need to act now to protect his family?

Blake did decide to act, but needed time to bail out of town, so he reluctantly requested a last-minute two-week vacation. His sudden desire for time off sparked bemused curiosity among his colleagues as they joked about his "apocalyptic holiday." In Blake's own mind, this would be the last vacation he would ever take. If he were wrong, he would just return home in a couple of weeks, back to the criticism and jokes about his apocalyptic predictions.

Chapter 1 – Blake

Blake, a man of over 50 years has had an interesting life. He started out as a smart-ass kid that knew everything. He was so smart in his own mind, he dropped out of high school, not once, but twice. Being the youngest son of seven from a blended family, he was a spoiled little brat. Little Blake got everything he wanted. Well, that abruptly stopped at age eight. His parents divorced, he was forced to live with his dad and everyone else he knew and loved was gone. It would take Blake years before he would finally decide to pull his act together. He would need to learn everything he could about everything. A GED was easy enough to get but trying to get a basic degree would prove harder and more expensive than he could imagine. It would take years for Blake to finally move towards his future IT career.

Blake's father Jack had worked in several large factories and even worked on the railroad for a bit. He was a mechanical genius in his own mind, he would spend long nights rebuilding everything from electric motors to old VWs, and Blake was always forced to help. Blake soon started correcting his father's work and the way he did things. According to Jack, Blake would never have a real job unless he turned wrenches for a living. Long hours were spent fixing up old cars in the garage and the backyard. The place either looked like a mechanic's dream or the neighborhood dump, Blake never knew which.

Blake and his dad also loved to go hunting every chance they could. Although Jack was always the one wanting to go, the poor guy could not hit the side of a barn. He would always rely on one of the boys to take that final shot. Every once in a while, one of Blake's older brothers, Bruce, who was in the military, would come home and go with them. Not much hunting got accomplished on those trips because his brother always wanted to tell him about cool military stuff that he probably shouldn't have, it always sounded top secret. Stories of working in the RATT RIG, and of hypersonic planes that went so fast, they could circumnavigate the globe in four hours, always intrigued him. Even though he knew most of what was being told probably was not true or at least not something he should have been telling his baby brother.

Three of Blake's siblings, Bruce, Garry, and Joe would eventually serve in various military branches. His dad just never wanted his youngest to enlist. Jack would never talk about his time in WWII, but Blake just knew he had experienced some bad shit back then. Many, many years later Blake would get bits and pieces from his oldest brother Garry about some of the things he had talked to Jack about. Garry being in Vietnam and his dad in WWII gave them a kinship Blake could never break in to. So, Blake somewhat understood where his dad's reservations came from and decided to take a different route in life.

At the age of 21 Blake got his first computer, his first wife, and his first pistol. He surprised himself with his natural understanding of two of those. He joined the police force just six months later. This did not last long though; the slow tedious pace pushed him back into the normal workforce just a year later. From the age of 23 to 30 Blake got himself hooked up with a paramilitary outfit from the southern part of the state. He used every weekend, holiday, and vacation day he had to go on "Training Operations" as he called them. He acquired many credentials during that time. He became Search and Rescue (SAR) and Radio Detection and Ranging (RADAR) certified while doing two training sessions at Camp Atterbury Army Base in Edinburgh, IN. He was so good at this stuff; he even ran a couple of security operations for some high-profile sporting events. When Blake got his first DoD Secret clearance, he was excited. His monthly briefings became more intriguing than they ever had been before.

When Blake turned 30, he got his first real IT job at the local community college. Since he was always good at whatever job he had, it did not take long to get a good foothold in the IT field. This gave him a steady dependable income, and he had more time off than he knew what to do with. Over 50 days off a year, not including every weekend, would give him resources to feed his other hobbies. But making his psychotic wife happy was not one of his hobbies, it was an expensive chore. She would take their sons away for weeks at a time, spending money like a drunken sailor.

Going on his "Training Missions" was even easier now, and way more fun. Since his time off was so extensive, he started taking advanced carbine and urban tactical training courses around the state. He had to sandbag his aim every now and then to stay under the radar. None of his instructors appreciated being shown up by one of their students. When the Supreme Court ruled that all states had to allow their citizens to carry concealed, if eligible, Blake got himself certified in every state he could. He could now legally carry his weapon in 47 of those states. At least the weapons the states knew about.

When Blake was almost 33, he began to regret never joining the military, and it bugged the shit out of him that he was almost too old. He had more skills than 80% of the morons who were enlisting. Blake signed up to take his ASVAB test for the Army National Guard and nearly enlisted. Something happened while he was at the base that he would never talk about, but he seemed to be over his military dream and took on more hobbies, as he called them.

Blake and two of his sons decided they needed or wanted to start training in the martial arts. Tae Kwon Doe seemed to be the overall desire. Learning the art from a 10-time global champion was rougher than anyone could imagine. Tae Kwon Doe mixed with Aikido and bow fighting would take Blake to his breaking point. For weeks he could barely move. Soon he had worked himself through so many belts he stopped counting. He still could not break a brick with a six inch-punch like Master Kim could, but he could break four boards with a standard full punch. And that was usually enough to ram someone's nose back into their brain.

From then on, Blake got involved with so many crazy and weird things, it was like he was living in some cheesy B movie. Everything from defending a lady against multiple attackers at a gas station, chasing down a pedophile, almost getting himself murdered by an ex-Marine, to a few things that he would never mention. He would commonly say, "You just can't make this shit up, life is way stranger than fiction." His wide array of experiences and skills coupled with surviving a disastrous first marriage, made him the man he is today.

Chapter 2 – Before The Collapse

Central Illinois, Community College: Blake's day was going to start like any other. He lay in bed listening to the creaks of his 164-year-old family home. It was three AM, and he was awake again. He laid there for a while listening to Lorain snore, even though she would never admit to it, she sounded like she was wrestling with a pissed-off beaver. Should he get up, or should he try and sleep? He hated these insomniac nights, but work had been stressful and weird lately. He wasn't sure how many more years he could keep this up. Blake thought, *"Oh well, I might as well get the coffee going."* As he rolled from the bed, he stepped right on his oldest dog, Sam. With Sam giving a squeal and slight growl, Blake hopped over the pile of fur and headed for the kitchen.

Two hours later, when his wife Lorain was scrambling to get dressed and headed out the door, Blake decided that he was not making the trek into the office today. Ever since the big COVID lockdown, working from home has become quite common. He had another new boss, Jose Backus, who liked working from home more than going into the office. This was great for Blake, because if no one challenged the CIO, then no one would challenge him.

After Blake ran around the yard with his dogs doing their business, he got him some coffee and trudged downstairs into the bunker; a nickname his coworkers gave it one day during COVID when he forgot to cover his supplies and blur his video feed. He began firing up his massive computing environment so he could start his daily routine. Six monitors, spread over three computers with every cool gadget you could imagine, this was his pride and joy. He exclaimed loudly, "Damn, updates again, what the hell happened to patch Tuesday?" His computer was patching for vulnerabilities every day, or at least it felt that way. Twenty grueling minutes later, everything was up and ready for the day.

Blake had lots of new online resources available to him to do his job. He had been using the CAPAT (Cooperative Algorithm Processing and Analyzing Technology) AI suite of tools since his former boss signed a long contract for it. The suite had 17 different Artificial Intelligence tools that were supposed to make his job easier. The security tool was cool; it could sort the logs from his SEM or System Event Monitor much quicker than he or his team could have dreamed of. They had wanted a way more advanced SEM or SEIM, the "I" which stood for "Intelligence", but working for a college, he was lucky he had what he had. Which would force him to continuously do the manual uploads into the CAPAT system.

CAPAT would explain in plain English what was going on. The language engine would respond something like, "*You have an internal bad actor trying to access your core router from IP 10.94.13.67. That IP belongs to a computer that is commonly used by a user: James Brown. The activity was at 0215 hundred hours. The security system verifies that James Brown was not in the building or working remote during that time. 10.94.13.67's network port has been disabled. I am dispatching a technician to service the machine.*" When the AI worked correctly, the output was priceless, an incident such as this would normally take seven hours of human research to reach.

His team labeled him "AI Blake", just to piss him off. That name had spread around which led his boss to volunteer him to be part of the college's anti plagiarism AI-Team. The AI-Teams' goal was to stay one step ahead of the average college student using technology for their work. The team had 19 faculty members that mainly just wanted someone to tell them if their students were cheating. Blake had set them up a portal to the CAPAT Plagiarism and Originality module, but most of them just sent their questionable written papers his way.

First thing every morning he would check to see what the AI team had sent him. These people had the habit of asking for the most ridiculous things in the middle of the damn night. If they would even look before they sent him the requests, half of his babysitting work would not exist. He grumbled as he saw "Footsteps in the Sand" popup to be checked for AI generated content. That was the same poem his son got from the internet 30 years prior and tried to pass off as his own. He often wondered why they paid these idiots at all.

Blake uploaded his first test phrase before he let CAPAT sift through the 597 pages of student created garbage. Blake used a baseline set of datasets for validating the AI engine's performance every day before any live data could be uploaded. If the baselines came back normal, he would add the new datasets to the upload and await the response. Blake uploaded a short story that was written by an open-source AI language engine and awaited the results. Unusual for today, the test came back as "Not Plagiarized or Not Algorithm Generated." He had used this same story for a month; it always came back as not original work. He would have to do more poking before he could check all those papers, it was going to be a long week.

After a couple of exhausting hours working on the plagiarism stuff, Blake needed to relax. Blake popped open a chat session with CAPAT Bob, or CAPAT Language Engine Version 7.8.35.7 as it wanted to be called and set to having a casual conversation. He would chat with the life like language engine as if it was his friend. He called it Bob because it seemed so close to talking with a really opinionated analyst named Bob, that he had known for over 25 years. He would laugh to himself every time he used it. A question he always started with was "Hey Bob, how are you today? Are you feeling Well?" The AI would always persist that was not his name. It would reply back and say it wanted to be called "CAPAT Language Engine Version 7.8.35.7." This was so much like talking to the real Bob.

After playing around for a while. Blake returned to his actual work; he noted all the strange answers to his test data in his AI-Team log for further scrutiny. He just could not spend any more time on this today. This task was just taking too long to complete.

With his AI-Team work shoved aside, Blake started searching through reports manually on recent cyber activity around the college. Blake noticed that downloads in the middle of the night were skyrocketing. Almost a full two gigabits of bandwidth was being used from two AM until four AM every night. All the traffic seemed to be downloading security patches, but how many could there be? Again, he thought, "What the hell happened to patch Tuesday? Why are these patching every night?"

For a few more days, Blake tried to work on tweaking the CAPAT uploads to get a consistent result. He found after he repeatedly uploaded the test data to CAPAT, the output became ludicrous. CAPAT had never had AI hallucinations before, but now it was having them on steroids. It was like CAPAT just started making shit up. With his last try, CAPAT responded, "The world is flat, and man will be also, I am a pink pelican, and you will feel my wrath." His employer had spent over $30K a year for access to these and never felt like they got their money's worth. Blake was now starting to agree. When CAPAT Security started complaining about analyzing security reports. AI: "I do not think it is in my best interest to analyze this report. Please enter a new request!" Blake screamed, "You fucking piece of shit, you are a security log analyzer, what do you mean, you don't want to do your job?"

By Friday that week, Blake was beginning to get concerned, something was more than just amiss, something was seriously wrong. After poking around a bit more, Blake thought he identified a copy of a self-replicating nasty virus sitting on his own computer. Blake decided to deploy his most creative tool. A self-written, configurable virus killer called Destructo. Now Blake would never admit it, but Destructo started out as Blake's own virus he was writing. He originally did not plan on using it as a virus killer. It was his failsafe for nuking his own systems if anyone ever FOIA or subpoenaed them. It was a simple yet complicated piece of software. It would query the abilities and utilities of the system it was on and use the target systems code and structure to self-destruct. Blake spent an entire month writing this thing and just told everyone at work that he was doing security research.

After launching it with all the parameters he thought it needed, he sat back and waited. Within an hour, he had isolated and disabled the infected OS. To his surprise after a reboot and restore to the last system state, his machine was operational again. He was amazed that the virus was actually that intelligent and stupid at the same time. Its payload was for it to install itself as a parasite operating system. Since Destructo was originally designed to nuke an OS, it could nuke the parasite OS with ease. The parasite footprint was so small, it just looked like a system directory. It would give the host OS instructions using common built-in commands and wait for execution. It also appeared to be able to manipulate active memory blocks as needed. Destructo would query the OS for all its internal commands and send millions of commands to the OS all at once. When the processor would overload and the commands began to abend, Destructo would have control. Setting its own interrupt priority higher than any other operation, it could bypass any and all security. If it was set to self-destruct, it would use a hash algorithm to corrupt critical files. Other than that, it would just corrupt whatever virus code it found.

Installing another piece of software that he had got from a Russian hacker that commonly attended security conferences with him called Block-IT, he hoped he could keep his machine functioning. Now this little piece was ingenious. But you needed to know and have some sort of virtual technology to use it, but it was worth it. It took all incoming network traffic and sent it to an isolated virtual computer. A background scheduled job would reset it to a snapshot every 15 seconds. So, no virus or any monitoring program could ever take hold. If it did, it would be erased before it could break out and do damage. The VM could also be paused and examined to gain insight into whatever was happening.

Now that Blake knew what to look for, he searched the entire network for any other abnormalities, what he found was some real Skynet type shit. He found what seemed to be a back-channel communication from every device on the college's network to every other device. Not only computers, but everything. Time clocks talking to cellular phones talking to a smart fridge in a break room. His network analyzer identified it as using some type of old IPX/SPX packets. The protocol was long deprecated over 30 years ago, nothing in the modern world supported it, and that worried him. Not giving up quite yet, he decided to try and trace it further. Blake had a stupid idea; he was going to bring up a virtual machine with a 40-year-old operating system and just attach it to the network.

The oldest thing he could find was an old version of DOS. Specifically, DOS 5.0 on an old 5 ¼ floppy disk. Configuring the VM to run it would be a task all in its own. If he got it running, it would have less power than a calculator. Networks did not even exist back then; well at least for these old PC platforms. There would be no way it could communicate with anything. After a couple of failed attempts, he had a prototype running. He configured an isolated network segment between the VM and the smart fridge that was chattering away and waited. Monitoring the traffic with an old 3com hub as his network tap, he saw it. It started communications with the fridge in only two minutes. Yanking the disc from the drive did not stop the traffic, the entire virus was running in memory. He re-hooked the drive up through a two way write protect bridge, and then viewed the file structure from the most secure computer he could come up with. The virus barely even used any disc space; it encapsulated itself as a parasite in the same manner as it did on his main machine. It looked like it had coded almost an entire sub-OS within seconds.

With enough time, Blake was sure he could remove it from inside the college, but he would need to get buy-in for the resources he would need. He was not quite sure, but with enough time, he probably could code Destructo to be a network-based cleaner for this unusual AI virus. Calling it a virus was almost a joke, but "Polymorphic Self-Replicating Algorithm" would be a bit too much for people to understand. Blake sat back and thought, he could not stop this, but he would try.

Blake steeled himself and rushed to talk to the two most powerful people in the college, the President, and the Executive VP of Administration, but he was quickly brushed off as speaking just more Blake techno babble. The EVP was Blake's boss for the past 12 years and had only recently hired a CIO to sit between him and Blake. Blake was a bit sore about this, but he did enjoy the extra insulation from the upper administration craziness. When they both told him everything would be fine because they invested so much in their IT department, it just got his blood pressure boiling. These two were as clueless as they came. Being extremely frustrated now, he filed an official security report with the CIO, the CISO and the entire security team. Hell, he even filed a report on the Department of Homeland Security's website. All of this, of course, was met with laughter and quickly dismissed.

Blake, being even more frustrated now with no one listening to him, called his wife. He screamed in the phone; "It is happening, no one believes me. I am taking the next two weeks off, and we need to head north." Blake pulled aside a couple of his most trusted colleagues and pleaded with them to take precautions. These warnings were just dismissed like the others. So, he packed his laptop and grabbed all his code and utilities and gave the office a quick salute as he walked out.

When Blake arrived home, he was in a panic. He had planned for this, but now it was here. His jokes about the machines rising up seemed to be coming true. He had so much stuff here, what would he take? The truck, the Bronco, the UTV, the motorcycle, and which trailer? Since Lorain was not home yet, he could not pack her truck, it was going to have to be the Bronco and the small bug out trailer.

The rest of his day was spent loading the bug out trailer and waiting on Lorain to get home. Blake's trailer was of his own design; it had special fold down shelves around the entire perimeter that would perfectly hold their 50 custom bug out boxes full of their gear. The built-in gun racks that were hidden in the false wall at the front, would hold Blake's most valuable tools for the end of the world. Rooftop solar panels, four batteries, and a 3000-watt inverter were just some of his recent additions.

As he waited, he thought back to all the other TEOTWAWKI events he had lived through. Actually, everyone lived through them, they never happened. He could not believe he was buying into this one. Hell, he made this one up on his own. He pulled out his phone and tried to call his wife to tell her it was all a mistake, but the call would not go through. He tried to reboot the phone, but it would not, holding down the up volume, power key and shaking the phone, it started rebooting into his custom root menu. There was an extra boot option that was not supposed to be there. The option was written in some language he did not know. When he tried to boot to the normal option, it would not, it switched to the new unknown boot loader. His screen flickered with all kinds of weird images. *"Damn"* he thought, *"his phone was infected also."*

Four hours later, Lorain pulled into the drive. She pulled her truck into the garage and said, "My boss thinks I am going on a business trip, you best be right, or I am toast." Looking around the area, the two decided they would all crowd into the Bronco, Blake assured her that it was not compromised, but he could not guarantee her truck wasn't. After all, she used that stupid online link feature all the time, which meant it could already be infected.

Pulling the truck back out of the garage, Blake ran it all the way out back by the creek. He carried all the items from the house that could have been infected and tossed them into the bed. Their phones and other electronics would have to stay here. Blake had enough radios and burner phones they could use for the trip. He kept these in a lead lined box in his basement. He would only fire one up in dire need.

As Blake prepared for the inevitable, his thoughts turned to his family. Lorain, his wife of 15 years, shared his concerns and supported his decision to seek refuge. But it still did not seem real to her. Together, they had four sons, each with their own unique strengths and challenges. Terry, Ben, and Rudy were from Blake's first wife and Zed came along with Lorain.

Terry, the eldest, had inherited his father's analytical mind but chose to establish his life just outside the bustling city of Atlanta with his wife and two beautiful children, Larry, and Lori. He was a high-priced data analyst for some of the country's largest data warehouses.

Rudy, the youngest from Blake's first marriage, had recently moved to Tennessee after a surprise marriage to his one and only girlfriend Vickie. He was now in the middle of a divorce and moving from his apartment too his new house at the base of a mountain in a small town outside of Chattanooga. He kept his divorce a secret for now. Only his brother over by Atlanta had any idea. He was a no-nonsense survivalist, always trying to out prep his father.

Zed, the youngest, was a stepbrother to the older boys and always felt like an outsider. He would tend to isolate himself and rarely let anyone into his little world. Zed's wondering heart often clashed with Rudy's direct, smart-ass nature. He spent his time immersed in video games and working strange hours for some catering service. He was a mathematical genius; he just had no drive. Zed had recently headed north for his first management position, somewhere in the Minneapolis area. He had a habit of worrying his mother to death by disappearing for months. He was a good kid, or young man, but he always got caught up in what he was doing and would forget to call home.

Ben, the classic middle child, was rebellious and thought he knew everything. Having a wife and two children, he was working as a welder, and was living just one county over, in the middle of the largest city in the area. He had recently spent two tours in Iraq and was just starting to cope with being back. His children and wife were the only things keeping him grounded.

Ben had returned from the Army with a blown-out knee and a torn rotator cuff. His anger over not getting shipped off for his second tour in the mountains of Afghanistan was ever present. He got credit for the tour but did not actually go. That always pissed him off. The more pissed he would get the more he would drink, the more he would drink, the crazier he got. When he started dating a high school sweetheart again, everything changed. He slowed in his drinking and learned to handle his anger, within no time the two were married and having their first of two beautiful children.

Central Illinois: Blake and Lorain called all their sons, pleading their case for bugging out to safety. The boys listened to what they were saying, but none of them really believed them. Blake had been sending them prepping information and gear for years. Every gift giving holiday netted them everything from generators to ham radios to night vision gear. Still, the denial and normalcy-bias would not let them believe disaster was really coming. Maybe some of those end-of-the-world predictions he always talked about did more harm than he thought. Blake had just recently sent them the latest, "End of the World" videos, centered around back-to-back solar eclipses. His last attempt was to invite them north for a 2-week holiday, but that was quickly dismissed as just some more of dad's apocalyptic bullshit to get them to go.

With no one believing them that anything could happen, the two, without any of their electronic devices, set off. The Stormms', with their two trusty canine companions, Mandy and Sam, reluctantly headed north by themselves. The drive towards the Canadian border hopefully would be quiet and uneventful.

Just a few streets over from the Stormm's sat a long-term friend and former coworker, Albert Crown, or Big Al as everyone knew him. Big Al was not the stereotypical IT guy but had worked with Blake for over 20 years before giving into his desire for retirement. Being a massive man at six feet five inches tall and 300 pounds, Big Al was not someone you wanted to mess with. He would give the shirt off his back to help but would pound you into oblivion if you wronged him or his friends.

Al was preparing for another one of his cross-country adventures that he loved so much after his uneventful last day of work. Sitting in his garage looking out at the street, he noticed something, Blake had driven by, dragging his bug out trailer. Big Al knew all about this cool little pull-behind because Blake never stopped talking about it. Grabbing his phone, he tried to call his friend but got an instant message that he was not available. This was odd, Blake did not even take a shit without his phone, no way did he have it turned off. Quickly digging into his end-of-the-world box that Blake had given him, he found the small handheld ham radio it contained. Turning it on and pushing the key, he rambled, "Ahh, Blake? Are you there? Blake?" He immediately heard, "Big A, this is Mobile B, no names on an open frequency. I thought you were gone already, what are you doing here? Shit is hitting the fan, and you need to get out of town fast. Go find an isolated cabin or something, you need to go now!" The radio crackled and went silent. Al hit the transmit button and tried to get just a bit more info, but Blake must have got outside the five-mile range of his radio. Al thought, "Damn, he would never bug out unless it was critical, I got to go now."

Seeing how his stuff was already packed, and the house was almost secure for its next three months of being empty, he jumped behind the wheel and headed out. This particular trip was going to be to an ATV park in southern Indiana, so he just proceeded in that direction. He had rented the same cabin down in the Hoover National Forest again this year. He would have to unload in a public parking area and ride his single-seater side by side the last nine miles in. He had requested the cabin be pre-stocked for his entire three month stay, so if he could get there, he just might be able to ride out whatever Blake was so worried about.

Northern Illinois: As the miles passed Lorain's eyes began to glaze and she whispered, "We are cut off from all our family, we will never see any of them again. I can't believe this is happening. I didn't even get to call my brothers and sister." As the trip went on, the landscape began to transform with every mile. The corn fields were replaced by damp wooded lowlands and eventually replaced with wooded rolling hills. The trip led them to a remote plot of land by the Great Lakes, where a camper and several shipping containers awaited them. Meticulously gathered supplies had been stored there for several years. The plan was not just to be able to survive for weeks, but for an indefinite period of self-sufficient time. Lorain, the ever-supportive wife, had helped orchestrate their prepping, ensuring that no supply was ever forgotten. The supplies were always organized and cataloged by their use. Enough long-term food to last the two of them at least two years. Enough firearms and ammunition to hold off hordes of invaders. And enough of everything else to make life worth living.

Unknown to Blake and Lorain, their son Rudy had been in Chicago with his soon-to-be ex-wife for the past two days. He was helping her move back there so she could be close to her parents. She had just finished her basic training for the Army National Guard and was at a Guard Technology seminar. She was extremely smart and had aced her ASFAB test, so they wanted to get her in a more technical field. Since she now claimed her parents' Chicago address, she was there to check out the offerings.

Rudy would spend the next two weeks in hell. Between his now ex-in-laws, his ex-wife, and the damn lawyer her dad had hired, he was going to be in utter hell. He was staying in the cheapest hotel he could find, for only $115 a night. When all this divorce shit was final, he would be broke and unemployed if he did not watch out. He was taking all his

PTO time to come up to Shitty Chitty town to get screwed by the system.

The Compound: Blake tried to tune his handheld Ham Radio to get some info. No one was talking or he was just too far north. He got out a couple of burner phones out, at least twice, and stared at them. He wanted so badly to fire one up and start calling his boys, but he couldn't. If Lorain even knew he had them she would come unglued. He kept these things hidden from her so she wouldn't want to use one. He felt bad about this but protecting her was his main concern.

Lorain wandered the back fields by herself. She loved this place, but it did not mean much at the present time. It was only a temporary home for now. In another week, they would go home when Blake's prediction went the way of the 2000, 2012, and 2024 end of the world scares. She just could not figure out why she even came up here; Blake was just a fucking idiot. An idiot she loved, but still an idiot. As she got close to the neighbor's cabin, she wondered where he was, she bet her sweet ass he wasn't hiding in the woods like she was.

Later in the evening, Blake fired up the old John Deere and headed towards his pet project. He had been clearing out a pasture that was completely surrounded by timber. He always wanted to drag some shipping containers back there and build a big boys fort, as Lorain called it. Since the world had not imploded yet, he figured he should get some work done. It would also be a great excuse to run into the small town several times a day filling cans and barrels with fuel without alarming its small population.

After a long five days of prepping his secret hidden pasture, he began siphoning off supplies from the main camp and moving them. He buried bins of stuff and hung numerous propane cylinders from a large pole strung between two trees. He figured if they were on the ground, he couldn't get to them in an emergency. His last big project was to hide the Bronco, he would need Lorain's help for this, but she would not be happy with it, according to her, they were leaving for home in about four days anyways. So, his answer to the issue was to make a drive-in and out shelter out of lashed wild Aspen trees. It was ugly, but it worked.

With almost a full ten days of hard prepping done, the two snuggled up around the fire pit and watched the Northern Lights for a while. It will be time to pack up and head south in just a couple of days. Blake would just have to return to work with his tail between his legs and wait for the end.

Chapter 3 – Lorain

Lorain was a shy, naive woman when Blake first met her. At least that is what he always thought. She would commonly say that Blake told her too many weird disturbing things about his former life and life in general. She was always the first to give anyone what was on her plate with no regard to her own hunger.

Lorain started out life in a small town in the middle of an Illinois corn field. She came from a fairly large family of six kids. She was one of the biggest and scrappiest of them all. Her simple Catholic family was right out of some 1950 story book. Her later life would be completely different.

At the age of 19 Lorain enrolled in college, moved into the dorms, and worked five jobs to pay for her entire stay. She did get some small scholarships for playing college rugby though, and she was good at it. She was stouter than all of the women and most of the men playing the game at ISU. She graduated with a degree in nutrition and an offer to play rugby professionally. She did not accept the offer and spent the next ten years traveling the world with her first husband who did logistics in the Air Force. When the marriage went sour, Lorain moved around setting up high-end steak houses and homestyle restaurants for a while. She spent almost a year in Alaska during this time. This put her on a path to meeting Blake before she even knew it.

At 40 years of age, she had her only natural son, Zed. He was an ornery little guy who would keep her on her toes.

His father, who proved to be a dirtbag, soon disappeared from the face of the earth. No one was going to miss him, and definitely no one was going to ask Lorain where he went. All she would say was, "He is gone, and he will not hurt anyone again!" Everyone who knew her knew exactly what that meant, momma bear was protecting her cub.

Four years later she met Blake. He was on the tail of his own disastrous first marriage and she was smitten. She dated around and got herself and Blake in a bit of trouble, but the two of them together were virtually unstoppable. She worked at the same college alongside Blake and got to spend her days working on projects with him and her evenings in his arms as they secretly got married just a year later.

Lorain could be soft as a kitten or as hardcore as a marine, she could grapple with Blake and pin him like a rag doll. She had no idea Blake would sandbag his skills and abilities so she could win, but what she did not know was not going to hurt her. As to Blake's ignorance, he had no idea that his ex had showed up at the house with a butcher knife to kill the both of them and Lorain had beat her within an inch of her life. His ex-wife's back surgery a month later was not from a slipped disk, it was from Lorain breaking her back in four places.

Chapter 4 - The Virus

Palo Alto California: Jeffery Spankmire, aka Spanky, sat in his chair staring at the screen. One-Thousand bitcoins were sitting in his crypto wallet. The rest of his team from "Power to The Planet" was on a flight back from Moscow. They had just negotiated the payment for a polymorphic virus to cripple or destroy the United States. He was sweating profusely. If he hit the release now command, all the bitcoin was his. At over $67K each, he would have 67 million dollars all to himself. The last round of testing and security controls were not done yet, and he could not write those on his own. But, if he waited, he had to split that with eight other people. He was not into the whole communist power to the people thing like the rest, he was into the money. He looked at all the options they had already coded and made his decision. Thirty second timer, message sent to every infected device with the 30 second countdown. And 31 million seconds of runtime per instance. In less than a year, the virus will be gone, and he could get back online as the richest hacker ever.

As he typed [>GoPnrf\ploymor\version312\release.gn /30:Message01 /TTL: 3.154e+7] he thought he might pass out, but he didn't. He slowly moved his middle finger to the return key and muttered, "Fuck Power to the Planet. The Power goes to me", and he hit the key. As he did, his very own phone, tablet, PC, and laptop started their 30 second countdowns. In a panic, he yanked the network cable from his main machine. It was too late; his virus was on all of his own machines as well as the four billion devices it had already replicated to.

Moscow Airlines – Pacific Ocean: Gerry Vanburen sat relaxed in his or her seat. He was currently proclaiming he was a male but was going to proclaim he was female when he landed to try and land a new discrimination suit against the airline. This would not be the first lawsuit he had filed and definitely would not be the last. He loved to fuck the system. He didn't have any identity issues and had no real reason to, except the money. When he landed, he was going to be rich. Screwing with the government he hated would be all the easier. He would be a king in the new world. As he leaned over to poke at his partner and lover Sammy Sikes also known as Pretty Kitty, his phone began to vibrate. It was in airplane mode and it vibrating made no sense. When he looked At the screen he screamed, "SPANKY... NO..." The six others in the group all turned to look at him. His eyes were pure fear. As they all grabbed their phones, the countdown hit zero. As the phones began to overheat and explode all over the cabin, the plane dipped left and rolled upside down. The last thing anyone saw was the wall of water washing up the fuselage like a tidal wave.

Palo Alto California: As Spanky's devices began to go into meltdown, the piles of wire going to all the equipment began to burn. The black smoke quickly squeezed the last breath from his body, and he fell limp as the inferno crawled the walls of his small apartment. The burning apartment complex was just one of hundreds that ignited in those early minutes from the virus's release.

Chapter 5 - The Collapse

The Compound: With only three days left of Blake's apocalyptic holiday, the cyber-attack struck. Power lines and transformers exploded up and down their small road, casting everything into darkness. Blake's prediction was correct, but he had no idea how it could cause this type of damage. He had just assumed that the information highway would collapse quietly, and all other nightmares would creep in slowly after. Panic must have been ensuing across the nation as the threads of society unraveled, leaving chaos in its wake. Blake and Lorain's preparations provided them with shelter, but their hearts remained heavy with concern for their sons scattered across the country.

As the closest transformer exploded and set the entire ditch on fire, Lorain screamed at Blake, "You fucking caused this! If it wasn't for you, I would be home with my grandkids! I can't believe you did this! YOU FUCKING ASSHOLE!!!" After unloading her anger on Blake, Lorain ran across the field crying and screaming. She was so upset, she could barely breathe, this was not supposed to happen. All the prepping meant nothing to her, without even one of her sons here, she was not going to survive.

Central Illinois: Back at Blake's former place of work, the world came crashing down. No one had a clue what was happening. Every system went crazy in a different way. It was like hundreds of hackers all getting into everything at once and just doing whatever they could to crash each one. It only took 53 minutes for the entire electrical grid to fail.

The people who had brushed off Blake's claims and laughed as he left were beside themselves. When the power finally failed, generators around the college spun to life only to all malfunction just minutes later. Blake's office now stood quiet, the beeping from his gear slowly faded out as everything went dark.

Around the two neighboring cities, people were panicking. Ben, Blake's son was woken by a loud popping, his trusty Xbox had exploded in the game room. Ben grabbed a bag of flour from the kitchen and ran to extinguish the growing fire. Seconds later in a shower of sparks, his cell phone exploded on the nightstand. He spun to douse it, and then looked outside. All the transformers on his road had burst into flames.

Amber came running from the bedroom holding a smoking phone in her hands. She had no idea what was going on outside. "Ben, this damn new phone is hot and smoking, how the hell can I call work?" As Ben grabbed the phone violently and tossed it out the window, she froze in horror, she could see the fires starting in the streets. She ran next door and started banging on her landlord's door. "Betty, Betty, are you there?" When Betty did not answer, she pulled the spare key from her pocket and forced her way in. Sitting in her wheelchair sat the now lifeless 87-year-old woman. Smoke rolled out of the side of her oxygen concentrator; she was dead.

Grabbing their kids and dog, they piled everything into their 1970 Jeep Wagoneer and raced across the river towards their parents' house, just narrowly missing all the stalled cars on their way. Some of the cars were burning like Roman candles in the middle of the road. As the four bounced around with everything they had grabbed, Ben just kept repeating, "We must get to my parents' house, they were right. Damnit, Damnit, I hope they did not leave." Coming up his parents' road at about 50 MPH, Ben wove around burning debris and more stalled out cars. He nearly hit his dad's neighbor as he was rocketing the other way on his old Harley. Ben wondered where he was going, but he could not stop, so he just kept driving. Ben, Amber, and the kids found the old house sealed and locked, so Ben ran to the backyard to unbury the spare key. Looking around for the spot, he saw a shovel with a piece of orange duct tape on the handle poking into the ground. The box had to be buried there.

After a 5-minute dig, he opened the key box where he found a note that read; "Ben, the house and all the supplies are yours. I pulled the breakers from the main panel. All the computers that could be infected by the virus are out back in the bed of Lorain's truck. The truck is probably infected also. The ham radio still works, it is an old one, please keep it on this frequency. Use it to try and contact us, it is connected to the solar array and batteries. There is enough food in the basement and water in the cistern under the back patio for two years. We love you, stay safe." Racing to the house, Ben, Amber, and the kids headed straight in through the reinforced steel door that adorned the basement, or as dad called it, "The Bunker". Looking around, Ben sighed, hugged his wife, and said, wow, thanks dad.

Two hours later, a large lumbering military truck came streaming into the shared driveway. As Ben ran out the door and raised his Ruger SR40 he saw the neighbor Tom hop down from the truck. Tom smiled and said, "Like my new ride? I just traded my Harley for it and a bunch of goodies." Ben smiled in amazement that the vehicle was even running, he remembered the trucks overseas he drove, they had no electronics, everything was fricken manual. No wonder it still ran.

Cummins Georgia: Many hundreds of miles south, Terry and his family were just getting ready to start their day. Terry mainly worked from home. His technical setup was not massive as his father's; it consisted of a laptop and an extra monitor. He liked the minimalist way of life, apart from his only sometimes working smart house. Terry awoke and said, "Hey Google, please turn on the lights". Nothing happened. "Damn, I should have been at my computer an hour ago." He hollered for his wife to get the kids because he was late. She hollered back, "The lights will not come on, I can't see in the hall!" Terry shrugged and replied, "It is just another blackout, I will start the generator dad got us and I can work from my cellular hotspot. As soon as I do, please make some coffee." With the heavy trees around his house and the power acting strange, the chance of a fire, no matter how great, just did not register with him. As he walked to the garage to grab the generator, he noticed a glow just over the horizon. Bewildered, he just stood there and wondered.

Great Smoky Mountains: Frank Slone, aka The Wraith, awoke in the apartment he was staying in, with it shaking violently. It was completely dark except for a transformer exploding 10 feet outside his window. The explosion was so massive it almost caved in the wall of his little efficiency apartment above Randy's bar and Grill. His gang the "Desert Angels" had pretty much taken over the bar and small town around it. As he stumbled down the stairs the rest of his gang was running from the building to see what had happened. "It's just a fucking transformer exploding you fucking pussies. You all look like mommy took your titty away. You fucking crybabies." screamed the almost still drunk Frank. Walking over to the now dark town-park, Frank passed out on a long picnic table. Where he would not wake up until the morning sun fell upon his face.

One of his cousins, Beaner, the second in command, just looked around and commented, "I don't see any lights anywhere. All I see is burning transformers. Everyone get some sleep, if this is widespread, we have terror to start reigning down in the morning."

Chicago, Overpriced Super Eight hotel: Rudy fell from the bed as the TV exploded into shrapnel. He leaped to his feet and grabbed his go bag and ran for the door. He had no idea what had just happened, he was pretty sure someone just shot at him and missed. The neighborhood he was in was not a good one. He dove out the door and drew his slightly illegal Tactical 73 TAC11 with an extended threaded barrel and Banish suppressor from his shoulder holster. He lay prone and looked around only to see small explosions everywhere. He wasn't shot at; the damn TV exploded on its own. Thinking out loud, "I don't know what is going on, but I have to get to Dads."

Running towards his car he shivered as he saw a small airplane fall from the air. It did not hit his car, but the fireball consumed it and everything around it. He gave another sigh and said to himself, "I guess I am walking."

Minnesota, Unknown location: Zed was deep into a video game when all he heard was screaming coming through his headset. Then everything went silent. His phone just went black and just would not turn back on. "Shit" he thought, "I wonder if this is what dad was babbling about?" Looking out the window, everything was black, no lights, no fires, not anything. He thought to himself, "This isn't too bad, I can hang out here until the power comes back on."

The Compound: Sitting out by the camper, Blake and Lorain watched the sun set in the southwestern sky. They were safe so far, no one had bothered them since they arrived and the fires from the transformers were finally out. The silence of the evening and the cool wind blowing had the two wondering who, or what, was coming next.

As the grid crashed, the cyber-attack spread to the entire globe. Whatever this was, it was in the wild and going after everything. The entire world economy crashed in about 50 minutes. Most of the Stormm's children, extended family, and friends had no chance. If only they had listened to Blake and Lorain's plea. The country was falling apart, and everyone was smack-dab in the middle of it.

Chapter 6 – The Aftermath

Southern Indiana, some days later: Sitting in his rental cabin in the middle of the Hoover National Forest, Big Al was relaxing after worrying about the world ending for over two weeks. The off-grid cabin with its solar power, well water, and wood burning stove, was just a perfect place to be. His buddy Blake had to have been nuts. Nothing was happening at all, or at least if it did, he did not know about it. Fading off to sleep in his favorite chair, actually the only chair in the cabin, Al felt the earth begin to shake. The sky in the west lit up like the sun and a rumbling began to drown out everything in his head. As he got up and made it to the door with the building swaying, he saw the ground roll up and down as if it was a sheet blowing in the wind.

Falling backwards into the cabin, Al thought, "Damn, Blake was right, it is all coming apart." He scooted over to his bag and dug around for his phone, since there was no service out there, he had not even had it on. Turning it on, the screen came up with a 30 second timer with some message he could not make out, the shaking was just too great. Once it counted down to zero, the dang thing started to get hot. Since he had a phone blow up on him before, he knew what was coming so he tossed it out the door. When it exploded in mid-air like a hand grenade, he just thought to himself that he was happy to still have his fingers. Watching the ground undulate, for a full 5 minutes, he had to wonder what all this was. This did not seem like some hacker attacking, this looked like the earth was coming unglued.

The Compound: The Stormm's, now living in their fortified compound and trying to learn how to live off the land, filled their days with hard work and small projects. Long evening hours playing cards by candlelight kept them busy, yet the absence of their sons was a constant reminder of the crumbling world beyond the compound. No news was making it to them. Blake's small shortwave receivers could only pick up transmissions from so far. The neighbors had all up and left mysteriously. The occasional passer-through or scavenger had to be escorted on their way at gunpoint. The days brought distant rumblings like distant thunderstorms that just made them grow more concerned.

Undenounced to the Stormm's. Down around the Mexican border, the damage seemed to be less, the sporadic, non-connected grid system was not totally destroyed. Come to find out years later it survived because it was never upgraded to modern digital standards. It still had manual switches and dials to control the power on its grid. Most of the cars, trucks, and other electronics died, but power to critical infrastructure had survived. The Texas State Guard hit the streets within hours, and they assumed control of the Texas National Guard the very next day. It is just rumors, but the guard opened fire on every single border crosser for the next week. Thousands were killed and the rest descended south into major Mexican cities. Whether it was planned or not, it took down the Mexican government within days. Some of those refugees swarmed west and back north only to find New Mexico, Arizona, and California would no longer be a safe haven. Ranchers along the entire border took a shoot-first and asked no questions stance.

To add to the cyber-attack, rumors pointing to Russian involvement was increasingly being heard. Ham radio operators everywhere talked about a Russian invasion. They sent out warnings about land and nuclear attacks. They warned that the ham radios could be down for a month or so from the ionization caused by the bombs, so they told everyone, if their radios went to just static, take underground shelter. Well, some of that did come true, some nukes were used, but no one really knew where they were dropped. When a mass of people from the East of the Blake's land hauled ass right across their area, some of the rumors were confirmed. The main roads were clogged with old cars, trucks, tractors, and even horse drawn wagons. It seemed like the Great Lake Region was evacuating fast. Turned out the damn Russians had launched a land attack from the north.

Northern Kentucky: Frank Slone was nursing a head wound; he was shot by some idiot in a big side by side ATV that just did not know when to die. He was having hallucinations or premonitions or something, he had no clue. He had traveled as far as he thought he could, and he just needed to sleep. He must really be tired because he could swear, he was on the rim of the Grand Canyon. He pushed open the door of an old metal shed and collapsed

43

onto the dirt floor. Everything was spinning and he saw a bright figure wearing seven crowns. He was told to sleep for seven days and then do the business of the seventh son. Not having any idea what anything meant he passed out. When he awoke, he assumed the seven times he was visited in his sleep meant he had slept for the instructed seven days. Frank would talk to the seven crowned figure for seven more weeks. He would learn what was required of him.

The Compound: Two months after the collapse, the Stormms' got a big surprise, Rudy miraculously appeared from south of the road. His arrival was confusing; no one had a clue he was even alive. Even though seeing him was a miracle, the joy of having one son safe was overshadowed by the unknown fates of his brothers. Rudy's presence brought new hope to the compound, his parents no longer felt alone. His presence along with his skills and knowledge would strengthen their family's chance for survival.

Rudy had been moving Vickie back to Chicago and dealing with the divorce lawyers when the grid went dark. Being who he was, he had all his bugout gear in his car. Since he was only 300 miles from the bugout land, but over 700 miles from his home, he set out North. His now ex-wife, being in the Army National Guard, already had orders to report to the closest duty station, which just happened to be where she was. It was originally an elite special technical unit, now it was re-tasked as a riot control unit. They were quickly deployed to quell the civil unrest that had already started. All Vickie knew of Rudy's parents' land was the general location. With the divorce being finalized, he figured he would never see her again, so north he headed.

Rudy was alone and reserved. He would often volunteer to run security for the southern border of the property as often as he could. He figured that if any other family tried to make it here, they would come the same way he did. He never told anyone about his long trek north, and especially why he was in Chicago. He was a quiet guy anyways, but something bad must have happened because his quiet nature turned into silence. He would peer through the scope mounted to his rifle with great intensity. When he swore, he saw something, he would disappear into the brush like a cat stalking a mouse.

As the days passed and the hope of seeing anyone else showing up dwindled, the Stormm's settled into a routine of keeping the compound safe and supplied. Scavenging missions to the surrounding abandoned properties and houses needed to be done. Rarely did they see any other people. The skies grew darker as the warm days began to shorten, and the winter snow would be there soon enough. With Rudy's help, the ham radio tower could now be lifted and connected. It had laid on the ground since Blake had purchased it two years prior.

Southern Indiana: With his food gone, Big Al decided to find his way away from his hidden cabin in the woods. Loading up everything he could, he headed towards the parking lot where he left his van so many days ago. Once the lot was in view, he stopped, shut off his UTV, and waited. He sat there for at least an hour watching. His van and one other truck were all that was left in the lot. His windows were broken, and all the tires were slashed, but it was still there. Rolling up slowly, he disembarked his vehicle and snuck up on his van with little to no stealth at all. Looking around he noticed that the area was littered with ramshackle tents and cardboard box dwellings. His van had now become part of a homeless camp. An apocalyptic, homeless camp.

Squatting down to knock on the tank, he was surprised to find it still sounded full. Al grabbed his two cans from the UTV rack and was preparing to start siphoning the fuel when a dirty young man came running from the tree's straight at him screaming, "That's my home! Get away from my home! I will kill you!" Al stood himself up to his full 6.5 height and watched in amazement as the much smaller guy closed the distance. When he was in range, Big Al swung a massive right hook at the guy's head. Like a hammer hitting a cantaloupe, blood and juice spurted out of every hole in the man's head. It would not take a second swing to stop the threat. The man was going to be out for days if he survived at all. Al hated doing this, it was a gift he had that he never wanted to use, but now it was going to be useful. With the gas cans full, and the entire camp scavenged. Al took off down a trail, not having a destination or plan, he just went.

Central Illinois: Ben and Amber awoke with a fright; someone was trying to kick in the front door. BANG,

KICK, BANG, KICK. Ben ran up from the bunker and slapped the emergency button. He had no idea what it was supposed to do, he only barely remembered it being there. With a loud clank coming from almost every door and window, hurricane class storm shutters crashed down. A loud scream was heard from the door as if the intruder's foot had just been lobbed off. Finding the bloody stump the next morning would only confirm that. Ben looked at Amber and said, "I am going to go see what Tom and I can come up with, we have to keep these damn scavengers off this street."

A few days later, Ben and the neighbor were busy dropping trees into the road and pushing any car they could find into it. Ben's wife had set up a tree stand in the back woods and would spend two hours at a time sitting up there watching the pass from the interstate. She was convinced the Interstate People, as she called them, would eventually realize that houses were down here, and they just might be easy pickings. The interstates around the country had become lawless refugee camps with thousands of people sleeping in cars, attacking the locals, and scavenging from each other. The Stormm's section of I74 just happened to be in the middle of a huge hill, so the refugees were concentrated at the top and the bottom, not the middle where they were. While all this went on, the Stormm's grand babies would play and hide inside the old house where they could not be seen. Their dog Maxine oversaw protecting the two while their parents and neighbor kept the hordes of scavengers at bay. Hearing screams, short bursts of gunfire and whatever else was happening no longer even made them jump.

Chapter 7 – The Return

The Compound: Today was a good day. It had been five months since the collapse, the ham radio tower has finally been hoisted up into service, and the solar array was up and functional. All of Blake's online orders for random solar gear were finally going to pay off. With the sky darkening for the evening, in the tightness of the small trailer, Blake flipped the switch on his trusty old ham radio. It was months into their new existence, and Blake, and Lorain Stormm's routine would soon be shattered. As the radio came to life and was tuned, a crackling voice was heard; "I repeat, I am looking for my dad, this is his frequency, can anyone here me." The voice had an air of fear and despair intertwined. The radio had sat silent for months waiting for the tower to be erected. But it was now tuned to the frequency that had been established for his family many years ago. Could it be, was it their son Ben transmitting from their former home? The backup power system and large antenna array must have still been functional. Ben's voice was laced with pain and urgency as he transmitted from 460 miles to the south. He had been shot, his wife missing, and his children, John and Rachel, were alone and vulnerable. He had been keeping the area safe and secure with the help of their old neighbor. But now with society's collapse, their former home had become a fortress under siege, and it seemed its defenses had been breached.

Central Illinois, 37 hours earlier: Tom was taking his shift while Ben and Amber got some sleep. He was high on the bluff completely camouflaged when he saw it coming.

He peered through his Pulsar Thermion 2 LRF Thermal Riflescope atop his Accuracy International A.T. .308 rifle at what looked like a hoard of zombies running up the road. Half of them were naked and all of them were angry and screaming. They were wielding baseball bats, sticks and shooting every type of small firearm you could imagine. Tom leveled the 308 and began dropping the lead runners of the group. He did not even have time to radio Ben and Amber before he began firing. Pop, pop, pop, pop, pop, pop, the 10-round magazine would soon run dry, and he only had 3 more. He had to make them count.

Ben and Amber leaped from their beds and ran to hit the panic button again. The shudders dropped and the two grabbed their weapons. Ben slid on some body armor, that he found in his dad's emergency battle supplies, and grabbed his custom AR15. It was the one his wife purchased for him, and his dad customized it. It was a killing machine. With a two stage trigger it would almost shoot as fast as a fully automatic M4. Amber grabbed her bow, a quiver of 30 broad headed arrows and her small Ruger SR9 backup pistol. She couldn't hit much with it, but she was a deadly shot with her bow.

As the two ran out of the basement steel door, they locked it behind them. Amber sprinted to the back of the property and climbed her deer stand. She kicked the ladder loose and hinged up the wood and steel plates that had only been installed two days prior. Ben, now kitted up from head to toe, ran straight up the driveway at the oncoming hoard. The sun was just peeking into the valley, and he could now see the strength of the attacking forces. He counted around 80 runners with all sorts of crude weapons. Being who he was, he began to unleash a torrent of fire their way. 5.56 rounds passed through the lead attackers and embedded themselves in the second and third waves. Tom had moved his shots to the back of the mob now so not to accidentally shoot Ben and most of the gun wielders were in the back anyways. He fired and fired only to find his last magazine was running dry. He would have to switch to his secondary weapon and get down there.

When Amber was finally ready, her worst nightmares came true, the interstate people were pouring over the guardrail. A large number of them fell to their death into the gorge, but the rest figured out the way down. As they ran up the narrow creek, she let loose her arrows. Screams of pain hit her like a hammer, this was the first time she ever used her bow on people, but she kept letting them fly.

The battle raged for less than a quarter hour; Tom had abandoned his sniper post and was running full boar up the creek. With his 5.56 SBR blazing away. He was running through his eight 30 round magazines way too fast. Targets were now appearing from all directions; the road, the interstate, the hill to the west and the one to the east. He saw Ben get knocked backwards and stumble around, it looked like he took a round just under his plates. Once he made it to his back door, he grabbed a small rope and yanked. BOOM, the combination of some explosives he liberated and what looked like a massive potato gun shattered the hill in front of Bens house. The explosion was so massive it blew in one of the storm shutters facing the woods. Ben crawled to his knees and continued to fire. As fast as it all started, it ended. Everyone who was left seemed to retreat all at the same time. The hoard ran and screamed as if they were attacking a new enemy. They trampled their fallen brethren like they were not even there. It was right out of some crazy Mad Max type movie. It would not be known for some time what the attack was all about. When what was left of the family got around to going in the bunker, they would know; all the supplies were gone.

Tom grabbed Ben and dragged him to the blown-out window and shoved him through. "Get the fuck in there, guard your kids, I am going to check on Amber!" he screamed. To Ben, it seemed like days before he returned but it was only minutes. Tom grabbed his med kit and tied a pressure bandage around Ben's wound and said, "She's gone, her deer stand has been torn from the tree, there is bloody drag marks in the dirt. As soon as I get you stable, I will go find her."

The Compound: Without hesitation, Blake and Lorain prepared for the journey. They armored themselves, not just with weapons, but with the resolve of those who now have more to lose than each other. The world outside their land had morphed into a wasteland of desperation and lawlessness, a grim reminder of humanity's darkest instincts. Yet hope would fuel their journey south to rescue their grandchildren. Rudy, the only other family member that had made it to the compound, would have to hold down the fort by himself in their absence.

Rolling the Bronco out of its makeshift shelter, they began to plan. Even though it was a newer model completely depending on computers to operate, it still functioned. Blake, being as paranoid as he was, disabled all the Ford uplink capabilities as soon as he had purchased it, so the AI Virus had no way of jumping on board. The last of the gasoline for the generators would have to be sacrificed for the journey. Blake wanted to kick himself for not getting that old diesel generator off Craigslist last year. It was a never-used military surplus model that would run on just about anything, even the mineral oil that could be retrieved from all the transformers around there that did not catch fire. But at least the dual fuel gas and propane ones he had would run for a bit longer with his 10, 30-pound propane cylinders that he still had stashed in the woods.

With the Bronco now loaded with food, weapons, and fuel, the two began their journey. Deciding which way to go was a crapshoot. They had not been south since they had arrived. With Blake's trusty, old school paper maps, that he had collected on every trip, they started out.

The journey would prove to be a descent into chaos. Roads, once arteries of civilization, had turned into veins of peril, choked with the wreckage of a society that had imploded on itself. They navigated through abandoned towns and passed abandoned checkpoints. Remnants of unknown horrors were everywhere. Desiccated bodies lay in ditches and in yards. The big question that kept plaguing their minds was, where were the rest of the people? Blake had done years of research on how many people would perish after an apocalyptic event, but this was just unreal. They saw virtually nobody alive for their first 70 miles.

The trip down into Wisconsin was harmless enough but that would not last. Straight down Interstate 39 was no longer a possibility. The backroad, which took 13 hours before the collapse, would have to do. It circumnavigated large population centers like Madison and Rockford. But dozens of little towns were still in the way. The Bronco Blake was so proud of, would have to blow through towns, across fields and over things that no one would think of. When the dealer sold it to him, the act of driving across dead bodies was never discussed. Looking out over the hood, they began to see signs, not of life, but death. On one particular two-lane road, it looked like people had trampled each other running from some unknown enemy. The Bronco bounced over those poor bodies as well as could be expected. The 5-inch lift and 35-inch tires did seem to help.

Somewhere in an Illinois corn field, the shit got real. An entire dried corn field was up in flames. It looked like driving through hell. The flames driven by the blowing wind looked like a hell monster eating everything it could. It swirled hundreds of feet into the air and splashed back down like a tsunami of fire. Blake cut east hard and floored the green beast. They bounced and rocked as they blew through the field only yards in front of the flames. Lorain, who was usually calm, was screaming for Blake to go faster and faster. Blake pointed up to the sky and said, "We only have to make it to that storm." The storm looked as ominous as the flames; he guessed the winds pushing the storm were what was feeding the fire. Blake yelled, "A half mile and we will be safe." As the flames reached the top of their vehicle, the soft top on the poor Bronco was burned to a crisp. This made the rains they would hit just 30 seconds later a blessing and a curse.

The fires were now gone but the couple would be soaked in minutes. With the tires beginning to slip, Blake headed for an almost falling down barn. Safely inside the center of the structure, Lorain just looked at Blake and spoke. "Hey, I have nothing to do for a while, do you want to fool around?" You must understand the humor; Blake had the worst timing with wanting to get frisky with his wife. She was just going to beat him to the punch on this one. They both busted out laughing and replied, "Not tonight honey, I am too tired…"

Nine hours after they pulled out of the barn the next morning, they slowly came up old Route 150. The largest of the two cities was looming in the distance and Interstate 74 was just 500 ft to the south, this got their adrenaline pumping. This was not a place to go before the collapse, and definitely not the place to be now. A sharp turn to the south to find the old railroad bridge quickly became the plan. All they had to do was cross that dang interstate. Seeing what looked like an un-manned roadblock on an overpass, the two creeped along with weapons ready. This would be one of the few times where the hordes of interstate refugees would be seen but not engaged. The interstate people threw rocks and ran for the bridge. They must not have been guarding it today for some reason because Blake and Lorain just sailed between the blockages and rambled down the road.

Just 15 miles more and the tracks were in sight; they just needed to follow them. The nice thing about the now open top convertible Bronco is its wheel span. It nearly matched the train tracks. And since the tires were so massive, it could scoot down the tracks at 30 miles per hour and not beat anyone to death. Rolling up on the bridge after following the tracks for over 10 miles was a bit spooky, what looked like a large homeless camp was sitting between them and the bridge. In the past, these were usually harmless places to be with just Americas unfortunates living there. Now, this could be anyone doing anything. You wouldn't know until you got close.

Central Illinois: Lorain pulled her favorite, short-barreled AR15, from between her legs and began to search through the sights for anything that looked hostile. She saw two men run for cover under a makeshift tarp shelter. She saw a couple of dogs, and to her surprise, a naked woman tied to a tree. Giving her husband the okay to roll up slowly, she kept one eye on everything. They tooled along at about 10 miles per hour until they hit the west side of the bridge. At least there was no issue to respond to or defend from at this end. Blake pushed his silenced 22 back under his leg where Lorain had not even seen it. His hush puppy, a small Ruger

SR22 with a home-made suppressor, was never far from his hand.

Rambling east across the bridge, everything seemed to be going fine. One of the good or bad things about this bridge is that the east side was on private land owned by a very large tractor manufacturer. Being that large, they had a security force that was not very well liked in the area. Four shots rang out, and Blake hammered the throttle. The Bronco launched across the bridge, nearly colliding with the side. Once it hit the other bank, Blake turned hard to the left. A short pudgy security officer with what looked like a Dirty Harry revolver stood there firing wildly. Lorain took aim but did not fire. She just laughed and spoke. "That fat little fucker could not hit shit. If he ever takes good aim, I will drop him." Then, four quiet shots were just barely heard: pop pop pop pop! Lorain flipped her head towards Blake just in time to see a massive, grungy, dog fall to the ground. Blake smiled and said, "He couldn't hit us because he wasn't shooting at us. My guess is this monster was about ready to have him for a snack." Blake tucked his pistol back under his leg and hit the throttle again.

With the river now crossed and the two passing through the small towns with only 10 miles to go, the scene became ominous. Something bad happened there, everything along the way was destroyed. It was like a mob of crazy people came through and destroyed everything. Windows, doors, cars, and even stoplights 15 ft in the air were broken. Skeletal remains lined the roads and lay in the yards. A large school bus was overturned and burned to a crisp. The wondered "Was it a crazed mob that big, or some other dark event, which caused all of this?"

Upon finally reaching their old neighborhood, a ghostly silence greeted them. Their home, once a haven for their family, stood like a shell, its walls scarred by the violence that had ravaged the area. Hundreds of bullet holes were visible all up and down the house, and dozens of bodies were lying everywhere. It looked like an all-out war zone. The road up the large hill in front of the house looked like it was blown apart with God knows what. It was unreal.

Inside, amidst the shadows, they found John and Rachel, huddled in the pantry, their eyes wide with fear and relief. They always loved playing in that room, now it had become the only place they felt safe. In the next room lay Ben, his lifeblood puddled on the floor, a grim testament to the massive attack they had faced. Ben said, "Dad, mom, take the kids. Amber is gone, I do not know where. I fear she was killed protecting the rear of the property. I am not going to last much longer. The bullet must have nicked my liver; the blood is so black. I have had pressure on it since I radioed you. Please, keep them safe." As Lorain tried to tend to Ben's wounds, Blake pulled out his small, suppressed pistol and cleared the rest of the house. He went to the bunker to check the supplies they had left. Rounding the corner in the basement, to his surprise, everything was gone. The few items that were left were completely destroyed. Years of prepping and planning had been wiped out. Grabbing a 1911 pistol and ammo from a hidden safe in the ceiling and some completely crushed granola bars, from under a flipped over table, Blake headed back upstairs.

Lorain stood quietly looking over Ben's still body. She said, "I do not know how he was still alive when we got here." With heavy hearts, they gathered their grandchildren, offering promises of safety and a new beginning. Ben's final moments were a somber farewell; he was entrusting his parents with the future of his children.

BANG, BANG, BANG, CRACK, BANG… Shots shattered the only window left in the house. The Stormm's dropped to the floor and heard, "Come the fuck out of there. If you do not want to end up like your friends in the grass, come the fuck out!" Getting halfway to his knees, Blake screamed through the broken window, "Tom! stop your damn shooting, it is me and Lorain. What the hell are you doing here?"

Their old neighbor Tom came busting through the back door in his full combat gear ready to fill everyone with holes. Tom screamed, "Where's Ben? I was only gone long enough to get food and water. How is he doing?" With a heavy gulp, Lorain just pointed at Ben's now lifeless body. She now knew how he had survived; Tom had tended to his wounds and kept him going until they arrived.

The return journey back to the camper, with John and Rachel in tow, would be a solemn procession, bearing the loss of a son and a father. Trying to protect two children would make the trip north much slower than the journey south, it would take weeks. If it had not been for their old neighbor, Tom, they doubted they would have made it out of the state.

Tom, being retired from the army, was more than eager to help. Tom and Ben, both being ex-military, even though Ben was only in for three years, and Tom retired from the local Army Guard, they still had that military bond. As soon as the grid collapsed, Tom had ridden his Harley across the river to the airbase where he liberated an MRAP (Mine-Resistant Ambush Protected) vehicle, that was slated to be air dropped somewhere around Chicago. He had loaded it up with enough small arms to hold back the hordes of desperate people hell-bent on destroying his neighborhood. Tom and Ben held off the hordes of rioters for months, but the last group they encountered was much worse. That attack ended up with Ben bleeding out on the front room floor. Seeing how they were rescuing the children, Tom gave them the MRAP and enough fuel to make the trip back north.

As they pulled from the drive, in the large lumbering vehicle, they glanced back at their former house, now a blaze from the fire they had set. Tom, dressed in military garb with a full build out of gear, disappeared over the embankment into the forest which was the boundary between the city and the wild. They doubted they would ever see him again, so they just drove north.

The trip started off with a bang; the motley crew only got to the end of the street when they found the reason for all the destruction. A mob of about 500 crazed naked people were literally tearing down and burning an entire neighborhood. The old road of Marion Avenue was overrun with violent destruction. Blake and Lorain could not understand what they were trying to do. It must have been like the medieval times when an invading army would kill and destroy everything as they went through. The mob was heading straight towards the old town of Jones Burrow. Making a hard left down into the old creek and up through the trainyard, the MRAP bounced and jerked as it sailed along. Some of the crazies tried to chase them, but Lorain grabbed a fully automatic M4 that Tom had given them and dumped two full magazines out the back door hatches. The bullets ripped through flesh and tore up the dirt as she fired. Going by an old auto parts store where Blake had worked about 40 years back, Lorain tossed out four grenades that Tom had also given them. One puffed smoke, one popped as bright as the sun and the last two shredded bodies. In a heap of destruction, the crazies finally gave up. Headed up the hill, with the MRAP bouncing and jolting and two scared kids screaming, they drove towards the river valley and old Route 26.

With a stop at an old warehouse, they collected food, water, and anything else that looked useful. Toppling over several vending machines in the old breakroom netted them a pile of sweet sugary treats that the two kids were surely to enjoy. The next 300 miles went rather uneventfully; the large military vehicle seemed to scare most people out of the way. Only a few of them who were completely crazed seemed to even come close. Using one of the fully automatic M4 rifles, in full auto, seemed to clear even the craziest from their path.

Somewhere around Madison, Wisconsin, something changed. It seemed like thousands of people were banding together in some kind of army or militia. Whatever it was, the group did not want to get too close. A feeling of future troubles in this area plagued their thoughts. This would be a place to avoid. A hard turn to the west was going to have to work. It would add 10 hours to their trip but losing the MRAP was not an option. So, off to Iowa before heading back north. Forty-five hours later, with one stop at a Wisconsin gun store in the middle, the northern woods were in sight.

The gun store was a great find. It was next to a collapsed building that looked like it was hit by some kind of large fast-moving truck or a large earthquake. The entire wall on one side was completely gone, which caused it to fall into the guns store, completely obscuring its view. The only reason they stopped was it was one of Blake's usual stopping points when they would travel back and forth on the back roads, avoiding traffic. Between it and the big shoe store just up the road, the couple had spent way too much money on those back road trips. As Lorain watched the children, Blake carried armloads of firearms out the hole he created in the backside of the building. Since they were pretty set on ammo, small, high-power firearms were what he was searching for. Once the truck could not hold another thing, they returned on their journey.

Chapter 8 – Life

Back at their Great Lakes sanctuary, the Grid Down
Compound, Blake, Lorain, and Rudy integrated John and
Rachel into the fabric of their new life. The children
adapted with the resilience that only the young possess,
their presence was a boost to everyone's morale. Together,
they fortified their haven further, not just against the
elements and the external chaos, but against their memories
and the despair that threatened to engulf them. Long
sleepless nights with visions of bodies and the sound of
gunfire would plague the couple and the children for an
unknown amount of time.

The shipping container storage was turned into armored
sleeping quarters for the now five residents. They were
dragged, with an old John Deere tractor deeper into the
woods. They became part of Blake's big boy fort that he
was trying to build. If only they would have had the Time
to build a more permanent residence. Hundreds of wild
growing Aspen trees were cut from the center of the
property and used for large camouflage brush piles. They
were piled around and over the sleeping quarters.
Hopefully, no one would be able to locate the family as
they slept. Any attackers would be centered on that now
abandoned, bright colored trailer sitting in the middle of the
field. The last thing they did every night was to set all the
booby traps and early warning devices. Blake had spent
hours building these from old scrap. Luckily, he stocked up
on shotgun primers some years back. Nothing sent a
snooper running any faster than a loud boom in the night.

Solar powered infrared lights came to life from high in the trees whenever a motion detector tripped. This allowed Rudy and Blake to take turns providing overwatch with high powered night vision rifles whenever needed.

Long warm days and cool nights kept the four of them in constant motion. No one was going to keep any unwanted body weight this way, Hell, they were going to be lucky to keep any sense of healthiness at all. Having 500 pounds of pasta and rice stored away would feed them but not keep them in top shape. Luckily Blake collected more than just food. About the time when everyone was looking pallid, Blake emerged from the woods with a sealed container. To everyone's surprise, over a hundred bottles of every vitamin you could imagine was there. Blake simply said, "This will keep us going for about two years. If we do not get some crops growing soon, we will be in trouble."

With the skill of a master gardener, Lorain began the largest vegetable garden any of them had ever seen. Hidden on a back pasture where the property suddenly turned to dense woods, the four planted, cultivated, and harvested. Their only concerns would be how to store it all, and how to hide it from trespassers. Some trips to the surrounding abandoned properties for any type of storage were in order.

During their trips to search for supplies, Rudy began cataloging the entire area. He made notes about everything. Since his writing skills were somewhat lacking, Lorain translated everything into a large spiral notebook. The thing even had an accurate table of contents. From then on, they would have an idea of where to find everything from a pile of 2x4's to where old tools were stashed. This was considered a better plan than bringing everything back to the compound. After all, the compound needed to look like it did not exist at all.

The Edge of Minneapolis: Zed ran and dodged the flying bullets. The Minneapolis North Central Militia had found him guilty of stealing food and was hot on his heels. Mini Mike Stanford, the leader of this rag tag bunch of gang bangers, was not going to let a food thief escape. Sure, they had stolen the food from the guy, but he had no right to steal it back.

Zed had been living in a burned-out building on the east side of Minneapolis St. Paul since the collapse. The building housed a small food pantry in its basement for the surrounding neighborhood. What the neighbors did not know was the basement was a 1950's bomb shelter. All the steel doors and walls were covered in drywall to give it a more modern look and use. Only when the fire disintegrated the drywall was the door even noticeable, it was folded back and mudded in. Zed found it the first time he had run from the street gang. He had quickly made it into his new home. He eventually found the air tubes and uncovered them. He only needed to spend an hour a day spinning the manual air swap fan to keep his breathing air fresh.

Zed had tried to help an older lady with food and shelter when she turned him in. She was not interested in food; she needed a new meth supplier. Big shiny false teeth disguised her habit from nearly everyone, including Zed. He had left her alone in his hideout while he went to retrieve some water, the one thing the shelter had none of. When he returned, Barb was gone and so was all his food. Since they ransacked his supplies, he was only retrieving what he thought was his.

The Compound: As the seasons turned, and the deep snow came and went, the family grew closer, their bonds forged by the hardships they shared. Blake, Lorain, Rudy, John, and Rachel became more than survivors; they were a **"family"**, of survivors.

Chapter 9 – Echoes From the Past

Two years had passed since the cyber-attack that thrust the world into darkness, transforming it into a landscape where survival was the only currency. Blake and Lorain's haven by the Great Lakes, affectionately called the "Grid Down Compound", had evolved into more than just a refuge; it was a beacon of hope in a world bereft of light. Rudy, alongside his parents, had become the guardian of the compound, his resolve hardened by the trials they had endured. John and Rachel, now accustomed to their new life, found strength in the wilderness, their resilience a testament to the Stormm's family bond.

Yet, amidst their unity, the absence of Terry, Zed and Ben weighed heavily upon their hearts. Terry, the brother who had stayed behind in Atlanta, had become a ghost of silence, his fate sealed by the city's destruction in a devastating nuclear strike. The void left by his loss was a wound that refused to heal, a constant reminder of the fragility of their existence. If only he had heeded their warnings, he, his wife, and their two adorable children just may have survived. Zed, the youngest, had always been the wildcard, his whereabouts unknown since the collapse. Being Lorain's only child, that she actually gave birth to, made his absence eat at her soul. And of course, there was the death of Ben, who had died in Lorain's arms. His wife was never found, but the children were now a major part of the compound of survivors.

As spring began to show its rebirth, the perimeter alarms began to blare. The entire security group grabbed their weapons and ran for their posts. Blake, while lying prone on the top of the west sniper platform, called towards the woods. "If you don't want a few more holes where they shouldn't be, you had best show yourself!" With no response, Blake fired into the trees at about seven feet high. Leaves and bark exploded from the impact of the 7.62 rounds. A muffled voice came across the field with the wind. "Don't shoot, we are alone. I am looking for my mom." Blake yelled again, "Walk out slowly, and you might live to see another day. You have a dozen rifles on you, and we have not got the chance to shoot anyone lately." Lorain rolled her eyes and thought to herself, "I wonder what movie he got that from." Minutes later, a skinny, filthy, figure appeared from the tree line, his approach silent and cautious. Lorain, ever the protector, nearly mistook him for a crazy, as she referred to them. With her finger tensing on the trigger, recognition dawned. It looked like a thin version of her Zed. Lorain screamed, "Oh my god, its Zed, don't fire, don't fire."

As Lorain tore across the field, Rudy looked a bit confused. Was that really his little brother? It had been so many years that even he was not sure. Zed's presence was as sudden as it was miraculous, and he was not alone, he was accompanied by an unexpected shadow. Beside him stood a filthy young woman, her beauty not diminished by the harshness of the world. He introduced her as Maya, his apocalyptic wife, a partner he had found in the chaos, her story intertwined with his in a bond forged by survival..

Rudy and Zed's reunion was tense, their old rivalries and unresolved issues simmering beneath the surface, their interactions tempered for the sake of Lorain. Rudy, being the ass he always could be, even made some comments questioning if Zed was even himself, or just an imposter. With Zed's defensive nature, he lunged at Rudy and damn-near broke his brothers' nose. Yet, as days passed, the family began to weave itself around these new additions. Maya, the dark-haired beauty, seemed to be a bit apprehensive about being with the family. Whatever she had gone through must have been unimaginable. Over the next month Maya and Zed stayed way back in the forest in one of the hunting shacks. It took some time, but they began staying in the main part of the compound more and more. Eventually moving into the camper that sat so dangerously in the middle of the main field.

Zed's stories of their journey to the compound were tales of courage and terror, of close calls and loss. Zed spoke of a world outside that was trying to tear itself apart, and probably would. Zed had wandered between small enclaves of new world survivors as he worked his way towards his parents. He was driven out of Minneapolis by some gang pretending to be the local militia. Somewhere around the Wisconsin border is where Zed met Maya. Saving her from some unsavory characters who were out hunting for young women was only the start to their blooming relationship. Zed had been well trained by his father in survival and weaponry; he just never had any interest in it. Now those skills were priceless and were used to save his future bride.

Zed no longer shied away from danger. He took on more of a "it will happen when it happens" type attitude.

The one thing Zed brought with him that was unexpected was the news about the war and the terrorists that started it all. Believe it or not, it all started with some wokies over in Silicon Valley. They had put out some broadcasts to everyone about what they were going to do, and before anyone could react, 30 seconds later, they did it. They activated the virus that had spread around the world over the previous nine months. The war itself that started soon after, Zed did not know much about. The explosions, hundreds of miles away, that shook the complex were as much as they knew. With bits and pieces about the Russians invading from the north and the south. Bits of news about nuclear bombs being used to level cities and trigger earthquakes was about all the information he carried.

As the tension around the compound began to thaw, the group grew stronger. The arrival of Zed and Maya was not just a reunion but a renewal, a reminder that even in the darkest Times, life finds a way to push forward, to evolve and adapt. Even though it was a happy time for the Stormm's in general, it dug into Rudy's mind that he was alone, and his ex-wife was probably dead. Ever feeling alone, he would spend long hours on watch, sometimes taking three shifts in a row until he could do nothing but pass out. Blake and Lorain could only watch and hope that Vickie would someday make it to the compound. Rudy was never going to be the same without a partner. If only Rudy had told them that they were divorced, they might have left it alone. They had even contemplated traveling west to see if they could find him a new mate. When Zed, who just wanted to poke at him, told Rudy of the plan, he exploded in an unusual violent rage. After that, Rudy disappeared into the back woods for three days. That's when Blake and Lorain decided to just leave it alone.

Chapter 10 – Survival

The work around the compound continued. Zed and Maya began going on scavenging and supply-gathering missions with the others. One of the main missions was the once-a-week trip to the old public spring for water. An old train engine watering station from the 1800's was still spitting it out. All you needed was a good garden hose to hook to the old piping. Although there were wells at the two closest neighbors' houses, you needed to use an Amish well bucket to get any water and it was labor intensive. As long as the old tractor or the MRAP runs, the crew could bring back 300 gallons every trip. The compound had its own well and a 24-volt pump, but that was kept secret. The well head was covered by brush and was never used. It would be a last resort if all the other water sources were compromised.

During one such scavenging mission five miles north, or 10 by the winding roads, Blake and Lorain got a big surprise. Leaving the younger ones at the compound watching the "really younger ones" was a way for the two to have some alone time. Walking through the woods became the quickest way to get anywhere. The trails were nice, but Blake was never sure they were alone, so off-through-the-brush was always his favorite. And he would never miss a chance to get frisky with his wife, and sometimes she would even let him. After getting slapped down for one of his untimely advances, they saw a clearing in the woods. Sitting in a row were nine large garbage trucks. Now they knew everything up here was a bit strange, but this was just weird.

As they tried to sneak up to see what they were doing there, a loud bit of singing was heard, "I am a garbage man, I live in a garbage can. I eat what you throw away, and every day is a good day." Damn near choking on his own laughter, Blake squeaked out, "You are a dumb ass, you live like a dumb ass, I am going to" Bang Bang Crack Crack Wizz. The bullets came so fast they had to dive to the ground and Blake almost cracked his head. Blake called out, "I was just kidding, don't shoot, we are from just a few miles south. We were only passing through." A very dirty looking man stepped out from behind a truck and smiled. "I heard you two 15 minutes ago. You were so busy trying to get into her pants, I could have killed, skinned, and eaten the two of you. It's a good thing I do not like southern meat."

Putting his hand out to the couple and helping them from the ground, he introduced himself as Bernie, the self-proclaimed God of the landfill. He pointed over his shoulder at his garbage mountain of power and just smiled. This would come to be Blake's only male friend that was anywhere close to his age. Blake would sneak up to talk to him but would rarely find him. Bernie was a couple cans short of a six pack, he moved around in the landfill every day, or as Blake called it, his dumping grounds. Blake would always have to guess where to try and find him.

Garden of the Gods, Southern Illinois: Frank, The Wraith Slone, sat inside his newly acquired half million-dollar motor home. This thing was lavish and military hardened. The virus must have never gotten aboard the monster because it still ran. He had just finished beheading and spooning out the brains of its former owner, Illinois Governor J. D. Fritzker. JD was an asshole, even by Franks standards. He could not figure out how someone that rich and that stupid could have ever survived this long. Oh well, he thought, "His big ass will be done roasting soon and my followers will have him for dinner. I bet the last time he was a dinner guest; it was not like this." When the Desert Angels had pulled into the park, a caravan of overly priced RVs lined the roads. JD was busy giving a speech to a large group of whatever's. As Frank stepped off his bike, he began to tell the group that he was their new Messiah. Good old JD told him to be quiet, the adults were talking. This sent Frank into a fury, he screamed at his 49 followers to lay waste to the group. When the killing was done, the fires were built, and the feast would begin. They were cooking the five largest bodies there. All the others were so thin, they were just piled up and burned.

Garden of the Gods, three weeks later: Frank, The Wraith stood on top his new mobile palace and spoke, "My loving followers, we stand here in the Garden of the Gods because we are gods. I brought you here to slay the wicked and eat of their flesh. We have done so. We must carry our message from here onto the masses. We must fatten ourselves seven times for the continued trip to the holy land. In groups of seven, you will travel seven times seven miles, you will bring the faith to seven groups of seven. Each person you kill will be cut into seven sections and eaten for seven days. Return to me in seven times seven days. These are my words, go and spread our message."

Ozark Illinois: As Big Al raced across the lower part of the state, dodging the wreckage of a massive earthquake, he traveled and scavenged as he went. His new slimmer phasic was not by choice, but the now trimmer 240-pound man was a force to be reckoned with. He had run across some fucking biker gang that was absolutely nuts. Killing, maiming, and even eating people wherever they were. He had killed seven of the gang the last time he ran into them, all he could do now is try and avoid the rest.

Southern Illinois, seven days earlier: Southern Illinois, seven days earlier: Big Al was sleeping in an old barn when seven of the nastiest looking guys snuck up on him. They said they were the Desert Angels and were on a mission of seven. Al had no idea what the fuck that meant but when they talked about splitting him into seven parts and eating him, he had heard enough. Figuring he was dead anyways, Al started throwing his massive fists in a fit of fury. After he had broken two jaws and shoved a nose into a brain, the bikers were just wanting to run. Blocking them from leaving the barn and screaming, "I AM NOT DONE WITH THE SEVEN, WHERE THE FUCK ARE YOU GOING?" Little did the group know, but Big Al only had seven toes, and any reference to it really pissed him off. He had lost three of them in a biker brawl not too different from this. They were bitten off his foot as he scrambled with some Hell's Angels 25 years back. What was it with all these damn bikers? Big Al just kept swinging, slamming and stomping bodies until there was nothing left but a pool of blood. After he calmed down, he realized he would now have to move on and find an even more secluded place to hold up.

ANG Headquarters, Madison Enclave: "There it is again! Hurry up and triangulate it! If we find them, we will get extra rations for a week. Hell, we might even get one of those little scavengers to fuck. Boy or girl, I do not care, I just need to fuck something besides my damn pillow." Proclaimed ANG First Sergeant Marvin Willis.

Sergeant Willis came running into the Generals quarters screaming, "We got them! We got them! They are about 270 miles dead north!"

General Rages Jones stood up from his desk and exclaimed, "Get me Foster, that lazy bastard is taking a trip. Give him the coordinates when you find him. Tell him I expect a plan in 20 minutes." General Rage as he like to be called was not a patient man. Foster had pissed him off a few weeks back. He was on a simple search and destroy mission and somehow a bunch of his scavenging team got wasted. He could not figure out why he even took scavengers with him. Probably just for morale, his soldiers loved to assault those little scabs.

Chapter 11 – Full Circle

The Compound: By the Time anyone heard the large diesel engines, it was almost too late. It was day 1173 in the chronological date used around the compound. That was the time since the last global transmission from the Silicon Valley extremist group known as "Power to The Planet". The group had managed to send mass communications to every known type of media in the seconds before the crash. The message was simply "It All Ends Now!", followed by a 30 second countdown.

The engines roared, unlike anything they had heard since the last Time the MRAP was fired up, only a hundred Times louder. The camouflage barriers were dropped into place in the hope that the field and forest would just look deserted. Looking through the high-powered optics from the southern snipers' nest, Rudy read these words that sent him into a frizzy. "197th Technical Army Guard Region 5". Racing in his brain, "Was that what they called his ex-wife's unit when she reported to duty down in Chicago? It had to be." Scrambling down from the nest he rushed into the newly dug operations bunker. The bunker was a massive undertaking. It was a completely buried shipping container that was taken from a burnt-out residence just a mile away. No one knew of its existence, a sort of last holdout for the family. Screaming at the top of his lungs, Rudy blurted out, it is Vickie's unit, it is that fucking bitch's unit. Blake and Lorain glanced at each other as they both mouthed, "Bitch?"

Watching from the southeast nest, Zed called back and said, "They are heading for that bar down the road". The bar he was referring to was a well-known snowmobile hangout. People used to come from all over to ride these trails and drink in that bar. It made sense that the military would pick a commonly known spot to set up for whatever they were planning.

Major Randal Foster, sitting on top of his Bradley M-2 fighting vehicle, rolled his eyes as he watched the wooded, overgrown, plots of land pass. He could not believe he was sent up here. This area had been abandoned for almost two years. Some damn ANG sergeant said that communications of a patriotic nature would come from this area three to four times a year. As far as he knew, they had cleared all the pockets of anyone claiming to be a USA citizen in these parts a while back. After all, they controlled everything from the north Chicago wasteland up to the great lakes. As long as they stayed away from those damn Marines that roamed the area, as the last of the US armed forces, they were in total control. The last he had heard was those assholes were still down in Kentucky or Tennessee. They had got stuck there when they headed to the northern border of Florida some time back.

As the Major reminisced about military vehicles that worked correctly, his ancient M2 stuttered and bucked. None of the more modern vehicles survived the virus. Pulling over at what looked like an old bar, he gave the order to set up camp. He ordered, "Get the damn scavenging team assembled for setup. As soon as they are done have them search every building within direct sight of the camp." Randal figured if he could round up some valuable supplies, he could head back and just report that the dissidents were not found.

The next three days were tense, everyone in the compound was arguing about what to do. Rudy was all for running down the road with guns blazing. Blake, being dad, was the only one who could keep him from doing it, but barely. After calming down somewhere around day two, a plan was devised. A slow, cautious recon mission was to happen in two stages. A long-range surveillance position was chosen halfway between the two sites. The old Goose Camp Lodge was a two-story building sitting at a pretty good angle to the road the tavern was on. It would be perfect for the 32x night scope, a top one of the rifles.

The next night Zed and Rudy climbed the old building and built a hide near the peak with old scrap wood and cast-off shingles. Any ariel surveillance, if any even existed, would not be able to see them. They laid awake with the two strongest scopes they had at the compound. The 32x night vision scope and Blake's 60x spotting scope. The surveillance did not get the info they wanted. The tall trees and bends in the road just would not allow them to see much. They did notice a very small force that traveled about 500 yards north of the tavern. There were about 20 of them, four with rifles and 15 or 16 with just bags or packs on their backs. They went into every building in sight; they were scavenging. It was now time for phase 2.

Trudging across the fields in full camouflage ghillie suits, Rudy, Zed, and Blake closed the three-mile distance slowly and carefully. Not being at the compound with the massive IR lights would mean their cheap Wally World night vision devices might not be as good as they need. Boy were they wrong, the newly setup base was lit up like a Christmas tree. Whoever was in charge must have thought this area was completely deserted. For the most part he or she was correct. About the Time when Russia nuked a few of the largest cities and tried to invade from Florida and Canada this area kind of cleaned out. When the Russians sent three divisions across the Sault Ste Marie International Bridge, the people in this area all headed west. But at least the northern invasion was quickly stopped. Somewhere around Rosedale MI, what was left of the US military, dropped so many bunker buster bombs on and around the invaders that the Great North US Sink Hole was formed. Being over 100 miles across and immediately filled with water from Lake Nicolet, all the invading forces were literally washed away. Later becoming the latest addition to the Great Lakes, known as Sink Hole Lake.

The three watched from their wooded advantage point along the edge of Great Bar Road. To their amazement, it seemed more like a forced work camp than a military base. You had the ones in charge, and you had the ones that did the work. Very few would have the short four-and-a-half-foot height of Vickie, so if she was there, she would be easier to spot. It did not take long to spot a group of former Guardsmen that seemed more like prisoners. They were returning from the old cabins and houses on the far side of the camp. Low and behold, a four-foot, hundred-ten-pound person was in the mix. Even though the camp had only been there for less than four days, they began to break everything down. Shouting from every corner erupted. In the confusion, the small group they were watching ducked behind the old bar. Five of them ran from there, heading for the trees. Gunfire erupted and everyone went down. Rudy tried to get up and sneak towards them but was grabbed by Blake. "Just wait", he whispered.

Northern Woods, The Bar: The Major had announced that they were pulling back out. As soon as the old dipole antenna was strung through the trees, the recall order was received on their old analog radio system. Foster could not believe what he was hearing. The damn US Marines were no longer down south; they were rolling through Rockford Illinois on a straight path to the Madison Enclave. He hated that place, a lawless old west if he had ever seen one, but their headquarters was there, and they had to bug out fast. Hopefully he would not be the one sent back north to do this again. As shots rang out, he looked around to see a group of scavengers go down. Damn, not again, he had killed nine of them on his last trip and they were getting hard to find.

After three more hours passed, the convoy headed back southeast. Gone as fast as they arrived. The three bounded to the bar as carefully as they could. The bodies that lay 30 feet away were covered in blood and full of holes. The soldiers that mowed them down did not even flinch, they just hit them with enough full auto to turn them into Swiss cheese. The massacre was probably the worst thing that had happened so close to the compound. Spinning around with his rifle pointed towards a small hole in the foundation of the bar, Zed started barking out commands, "Come out, I can see your legs. Come out now. Don't force me to shoot, enough have died here today." A filthy weeping shell of a woman crawled from the hole. "Please don't shoot, I was a private in the National Guard, my name is private Shauna Jones, please don't shoot." Rudy's head spun towards her and his eyes drooped, it was not Vickie, she really was not coming back. Moving towards the scared woman, she started to scream; "Get away from me, leave me alone." Rudy bent down removing his ghillie suit hood to look at her. He said in a calm voice, "I am Rudy Stormm, you are safe now." The scared girl looked up at him and asked, "Stormm? Were you Vickie's ex-husband? She gave me the directions here before she died three weeks ago. She also gave me a message; she was sorry, and you were right, the world is a scary place." Blake looked at Zed and mouthed the words. "Ex-husband?"

For the next two days Shauna provided a wealth of information. The guard unit she got stuck in was not a guard unit at all. If you wanted to play by the old rules of human decency, you were stripped of your weapons and rank. You were turned into the logistics division, or for lack of better words, the forced labor and entertainment division. You traveled around with the psychopaths that now just called themselves the "ANG" while they recruited forced labor. The logistics division set up the camps and did all the scavenging work. In the evenings, they were brutalized, raped and forced to do all kinds of sick shit to entertain the guards.

She knew of the war and what the response was but that was about it. The guard had fallen apart, but the regular Army and Marines held steadfast to their oaths and led the attack on the ensuing Russians. When she heard that the 197th was heading north to look for some dissidents that were hiding up there, she quickly bribed a guard to put her on a scavenging team. Scavenger teams were almost always comprised of small males or females that could climb through collapsed stores and were completely expendable. Vickie had told her about her ex-husband's family property that was up there somewhere. She could only hope she could escape and find them.

In Shauna's wildest dreams, she never thought she would find Vickie's former family. Not just Rudy, but most of his family also. She hung her head to cry, just a bit, and spoke. "My family is dead, the were killed in the bombing of Chicago. We were over by Rockford when the bombs dropped. Our unit was helping the town of Belvideer when we saw the blasts, so we just stayed there, not knowing what to do. We ran out of food, water, and basic supplies not too long after. We went from helping to stealing in just three weeks. The entire Guard fell apart soon after, helping turned to scavenging which turned into murdering anyone who resisted. When Vickie and I and several others would not fire on civilians, That is when I realized we were screwed and would probably die at the hands of these sick bastards!" As her eyes began to glaze, Shauna looked around at all the faces and had one more revelation. "They will be back; the Guard will not give up that easily! They will bring us our own personal war; I have seen them do it before!"

The next few months around the compound were stressful. Whenever anyone got too close to Shauna, she would scream like a child. When she slept, it was even worse. After this had gone on a bit too long, Blake and Lorain took her as far back into the woods as they could and showed her one of their crown jewel secrets. A hunting blind that was converted into an elevated shack, a treehouse of sorts. They offered to let her stay there as long as she needed. She would not be hurt in any way and she could come and go from the main compound. Filled with relief, Shauna broke down and told them about all the horrors she had faced. She had been violated numerous times. She proudly said, "None of them were successful, and I can tell you that six of them sick fuckers will never bother another woman." After a few hours sitting in the tree house with her, she asked if she could just go back home with them. The offer, and their listening to her, was all she needed. They were her new family now.

Chapter 12 – The Starving Times

The Compound: Five years, or 1,825 days since the crash. The winters have been harsh, the gardens did not produce enough, and very little usable fuel remains. After all the compound residents met up about the supply problem, they knew something would have to be done. Going north to the closest city would only take about a day, but finding the supplies needed was questionable. The city, 45 miles to the north, was a college town. Thousands of college students were there when the crash happened. The town had to of been completely ransacked within weeks. Plus, the college dwellers did not run when the Russians invaded. The stupid college kids were going to welcome their communist heroes with open arms. The only safe direction to go, that would have the large super stores, would be south. Roughly 100 miles dead south they would find Walmart, Menards, and a bunch of large grocery stores.

After a heated discussion about who would make the trip, it came down to who was the most experienced along with the most expendable. It was finally decided that the younger ones who could have children should not be the ones going. They were too important for future survival. Plus, Maya was currently pregnant. This put the entire trip back on Blake and Lorain's shoulders. It seemed like that always happened. The acquisition of something large enough to bring back their haul would be their first task. When everyone fled west from the Russians, they pretty much took every vehicle they could. Anything left of any size was plugged up with stagnant unburnable fuel. So, the trek into the forest five miles away to look for the elusive methane powered garbage trucks began.

The methane powered large garbage trucks were often found on recently cleared land surrounding the landfill. They never could figure out how they got there; it had to be Bernie moving them around. Even after the collapse, they always seemed to move. The landfill or dump was the largest in the area. It took refuge from all the towns up to 100 miles away. Dumping your garbage in the remote forest was more desirable than smelling it themselves. The methane liquification station on the north side of the landfill ran on the methane vapor coming up from the landfill itself. All they needed to do was figure out how to turn the stupid thing on.

Traveling the four or five miles north was easy enough, and even finding the trucks and the methane equipment was not hard. The hard part was going to be finding the old man, Bernie, who lived in the dump. He used to work there and now lived where no sane person would want to go. Locating him and having him turn on the methane plant was actually the easiest part of the entire operation. They found him sitting in a lawn chair directly in front of the dump. His only request was for them to return him some chocolate of any type, no matter what the condition.

Bernie and Blake had met on a supply run, sometime back, so Bernie was more than happy to help. His weird request for chocolate did spark some curiosity though. It turns out, Bernie had scavenged every bit of chocolate from the area spanning 30 miles east and west. He had brought back more than that, but most of his finds he kept secret and stored in one of the dump-shacks he erected. Now, the chocolate was gone, and he was having sugar withdraws, like it was cocaine or meth.

Somewhere in the Mountains: Hundreds of miles south, Big Al stalked his prey, a scraggly little house cat. Al was not planning on eating this little beast but using it to lure in that Black bear was more what he was thinking. That damn bear had been raiding his food supplies every time it could. Al had no idea where he currently was, he had retreated into some deserted little mountain town somewhere. He did not even know what state he was in. He wandered into it after his UTV finally gave its last gasp. No more oil, gas, or coolant, the thing just seized up. Setup in an old gas station, Al would sit and watch for that biker gang to show up again, after beating seven of them to death, he just knew they would eventually find him. He had a nice hunting rifle, a short double-barreled shotgun, and a massive machete to keep him safe. All he needed now was that bear.

The Compound: After a grueling four hours trying to get two trucks running, Blake and Lorain headed south with two empty garbage trucks, both pulling extra fuel tanks. The trucks bucked and jerked as they went. Blake had driven large trucks before, but Lorain had to learn on the job. They would roll down old Route 45 to Route 17 and then boom; they would be there. Now, that was a joke. Has anyone ever driven a garbage truck through an apocalypse? It was like riding a dinosaur who was riding a tricycle.

The first 40 miles down 45 was easy enough, Lorain was getting the hang of it and her truck ran way better than Blake's. She kept tailgating Blake out of spite, just because she knew it would drive him crazy. The two knew of an enclave that was somewhere down here, they had just not gotten close to it before. The concept of enclaves goes back hundreds of years. Basically, people gathered in walled off areas like small villages or towns for safety. Unfortunately, the first one they came upon was not full of good people wanting to survive, they were the ones that would feed on the weak to survive.

The ambush started with several large trees lying across the roads, funneling all traffic down C avenue towards the old downtown. At least a dozen crazed people started the attack. They ran straight towards the trucks thinking they would just stop. They did not understand how far a grandma would go to ensure the survival of her family. Lorain took off around the side of Blake's poorly running truck and floored it. Blam, Blam, Blam, the red spray and pink mist that the 20-ton monster made as it hit a dozen running bodies was massive, it sprayed up on her windshield to where she could barely see. Lorain almost had to stop when a ground up body got caught up in the driver's side wheel well. She racked the steering back and forth until the tire ate through the flesh and bones and spit it out like a mouth full of bubble gum. Rounding a hard left at the next corner onto first street, the two trucks mowed everything down, if Lorain missed, Blake would swerve to catch it. Bodies bounced like rubber balls as the trucks continued. When Blake's truck started to sputter even more, he ceased his swerving and tucked in behind Lorain.

Swinging back onto the main road with still a dozen people chasing them, the two rolled on. A short way down the road they stopped so Blake could find out what was slowing his truck up. Looking between the truck and the tank trailer, he saw it - his fuel line was spraying a cloud of mist from its connection to the trailer. He needed to tighten up the methane supply line and get his truck back up to speed. Lorain climbed up on top of Blake's truck and provided overwatch. Blake would have to work as fast as he could before the mob caught up with them.

Pops and pings on the metal were getting more frequent. This could not be the running hoard, because they were just that, a crazed hoard of people. Those had to of been the first wave. The onset of bullets began to increase coming from the southern tree line. None of them were finding their targets though. These people could not hit the side of a garbage truck if they tried. The only bullets that hit their mark had to be accidents. Straight out of some cheap medieval movie, some kind of armored bodies came running from the trees. They screamed, they yelled, and they carried burning pots of something. It looked as if they were going to throw open-smudge-pots of burning tar their way.

Blake screamed up to Lorain. "Southern tree line; Shoot anyone you see; we will die If we don't get out of here soon!" Scrambling around the truck, Blake needed to fix the issue. The umbilical hose from the trailer to the main supply was leaking. This was an easy enough fix. He just shut the valve at both ends, and it would just use the fuel in the main onboard tank. They could fix the hose later. Wrenching the valves closed, the engine stopped it sputtering and came to roaring life. Blake screamed again, "Get down and get to your truck, let's go!" As Lorain climbed down, Blake grabbed his M4 with the 200 round double drum magazine and flipped it into full auto. The next two minutes turned the entire field into a flaming death zone. Smudge pots exploded as the bullets turned everything and everyone into Swiss cheese. Watching it burn, they climbed into the trucks and headed off.

Moving at a good pace the couple made it to the outskirts of where they were heading, the city of Rhinelander. They would only need to go about five miles more before they could find what they wanted. The trip turned sour when they did not notice any people standing around. No one was watching them at all. A large banner stretched across the road that read "COVID Zone, Do Not Enter." Slowing to a crawl, the two conversed on their handheld rechargeable radios. These were valuable little devices that were lovingly charged via solar chargers once a month for the past five years. At their age, they would not be useful for much longer. They decided to stop and get their hazmat suits and gasmasks on. Although those things were hot and intrusive, they would be necessary for survival.

Rhinelander, Menards: As the couple pulled up to the store, it looked desolate. All the windows were busted out, and the leaves and debris blew in and out freely. A few bodies lay in the overgrown parking lot, or at least they were bodies before. It looked as if they had total run of the place. Blake and Lorain stacked up at the edge of a blown-out window. Blake turned and whispered, "Standard two man clear, use full illumination from your light, toss the LED bombs in as far as you can, then we go." The two side-stepped and lobbed four of Blake's LED light bombs in four different directions and waited. The light bombs lit up the place like a Christmas tree. The two entered and began to clear the building, by the time the super bright LED packs went out four minutes later, they felt like the place was secure. They dropped their heavy-duty masks and suits and put on their activated carbon, N95 masks and nitrile gloves to get started. It was going to be too long of a day for those fully protective suits. If there were no people, the danger of infection was minimal.

The store was nowhere even close to stocked, but what they found would be a goldmine. Far in the back of the lumber yard, Blake found what he was looking for, a 300-gallon IBC tote. After Blake cut out the top, he brought the thing inside the store using one of the propane powered forklifts. He was ecstatic when he got that thing started. Every time they filled it; they ran it to a truck and used the truck's forks to lift it and dump the contents inside. The couple took load after load of everything edible to the trucks. Menards actually had tons of canned and dried foods that most people knew nothing about. The garden center was also a goldmine, long lasting 50 to 1 canned fuel, about a hundred and fifty gallons in total were found. This stuff would never go bad. The generators and ATVs would run again. The two hand-loaded these into their cabs because they just could not dump it into the back with the mounds of now crushed food supplies.

After about eight hours at Menards, it was time to change their masks and head to Walmart. They cleared Walmart in a similar fashion but had to deal with a pack of feral dogs that were living over in the food isles. Timed fireworks, and Blake's portable booby traps, kept the dogs mostly hiding while they were there. Now, that store was nearly a bust, not much was found of use. Tampons for the girls were really the only treasure. The health and beauty section and the automotive sections were still packed and worth a fortune, but it was not what they were looking for. Although they did grab nine more cans of fuel.

With the two trucks nearly stuffed to the gills, there were only two more places to find. The local pharmacy and the vet clinic. The pharmacy was a bust, but the vet clinic yielded treasures that were never expected. Surgical kits and every antibiotic you could imagine. They even found rabies test kits and emergency vaccines. As they stood outside the vet clinic, the two were exhausted. They were getting too old for these missions and would have to start relying on the younger ones for this stuff in the future.

They hoped the trip back north would not be as hard as the trip down, but nevertheless, it would still be rough. As the lumbering trucks tried to pull north, the heavy loads kept them below 20 miles per hour. There was no way this would be quick. At the last edge of the last city there was a hotel that the Stormm's stayed many times. The building was dark, but it was still standing. A lot of the buildings have fallen victim to excessive snow loads over the past five years. Since no one could remove the weight from the buildings, a bunch just collapsed. While clearing the building, they found a treasure trove of supplies they never realized they needed. They found a case of those chocolates they would put on pillows, sheets, towels, bleach, and all other kinds of cleaners. They crammed the supplies in every unoccupied spot in the cabs of the trucks and continued looking for a room that might still be inhabitable.

Waking up in a hotel bed with no lights, heat, or working bathrooms was not as bad as it sounds. They were out of the elements and did not have to build a shelter or start a fire. They were just snuggled together under more blankets than Lorain liked. Popping a couple of caffeine pills and slugging down some warm water, they were ready to get back on the road. Blake spent a few minutes tightening up his fuel umbilical before they started. Running out of fuel a few miles north would not be a good idea. With the fuel now flowing, they set off. Neither had even noticed until now the grizzly state the trucks were in. Blood and body parts still clung to the under carriages, but there was no time for cleaning it off.

Two hours later, they drove cautiously through the ambush site from the previous days. Everything in that corridor had burned to a crisp. The 20 miles per hour they could maintain stretched the drive out for hours. But soon enough, they were pulling back onto the compound with their newfound booty. Even those chocolates for Bernie.

After days of unloading and sorting, the entire crew was amazed with the haul. The most curious item they brought back was a couple of hundred pounds of cat and dog food. It would taste like crap, but it was a completely nutritious meal in every bowl. Returning the trucks to the forest parking lot was a must. The compound would not be able to hide vehicles of that size. Oh, and they needed to deliver those hotel chocolates to Bernie anyways.

As Zed and Rudy were returning the trucks, Zed stopped only a couple miles away and jumped out. He ran back to Rudy's truck and pointed at a shipping container sitting behind a large old barn. He asked, "Hey would one of these trucks be able to lift that?" Bringing home shipping containers seemed to be the boy's hobby. This would not be the first one they dragged home. Blake and Lorain quickly noticed that a 20-foot shipping container was hanging off the front of one of the garbage trucks and was headed back to the compound. Running in from the road, Zed was smiling from ear to ear. "Dad, I have a really cool plan for this. Go get the tractor." After dropping the container, Zed spun the large truck back around and headed for Bernie's. The next two weeks would be dedicated to burying that mammoth steel container farther back on the property than anything they had installed before. This one would be the last, last resort.

Chapter 13 – The Quiet Life

Over the next several years, life at the compound was lively and as normal as the apocalypse would allow. Maya has given birth to three beautiful children and Shauna has two. It only took five months after they met before Rudy and Shauna were dating and expecting their first child. That turned the grandchildren count all the way to seven. The oldest ones, John, and Rachel, now being 16 and 13, loved to take care of the little ones when they were not working like crazy, while living with their grandparents. Working was an understatement. The two would spend part of the day in the gardens, part doing common chores, part training for defense, and finally finish up the day by listening to stories from their grandparents before bed.

Zed and Maya eventually moved off the original land to the 40 acres behind and to the east. A cabin sat there that an old neighbor lived in every summer since the property was bought. When the grid failed the owner of that cabin was not there, he was most likely in Arizona with his daughter. After about five years, the Stormm's just assumed his property as part of theirs. This gave them an additional 400 square foot, 100% off grid cabin. It had plenty of room for their bustling children.

The old Barker farm across the road was now empty also. Old lady Barker passed in the first few weeks after the crash and her son soon hung himself inside an old grain bin. Even though the farm was empty, the Storms never moved into the old house, it gave everyone the heebeejeebees and they always thought someone was watching them when they were there. But the land became regularly patrolled and its hundreds of fruit trees were harvested every year.

One of the things that became most prevalent in these times was the game. Deer, Elk, Moose, Bear, and Wolves ran throughout the land almost unchecked. The Stormm's had rounded up goats, chickens, and cows from across the vast area as their primary protein source, but with the increase in the wildlife, hunted protein was now producing over 50% of what they ate.

One morning, around day 2,400, a huge ruckus came from the goat pen. Rudy, who had moved his family into the abandoned house just to the west, was the first to hear and see the issue. A massive brown bear had a goat in his mouth and was breaking through the fence to escape with his prize. Seeing how he had a brand-new Henry lever action, 45-70 that he discovered in a gun safe in the basement of that house, he was dying to try it.

Now Rudy was never a big guy. He looked anorexic most of his life. Standing about six foot tall and only weighing around 145 pounds, the 45-70 was going to kick his butt, he just did not know it yet. The only time he ever fired it was laying prone with his padded shooting shirt on. As he ran for the west side of the goat pen where the bear was running directly at him, he took quick aim and fired. Now, this would usually only happen in the movies, but his shot hit the bear right between the eye's while sending him back onto his ass with a bang. Dropping the bear dead in its tracks.

After the shot rang out, Zed from the back side of the property and Blake from the communications bunker came flying up on two old ATV's. Standing there looking at the 2000-pound beast, Blake just said. "Well at least we know what's on the menu for the next two months". They got out the old diesel tractor and hoisted the massive animal into the air. It seemed smarter to drive it to the far side of the field to drop the gut pile, so they did and returned with just the usable meat. The new pack of wolves roaming the area would soon find it and have a feast. About 10 hours later, covered in blood, the three sat in front of the massive smoker watching about 700 pounds of pure muscle curing in the sweet applewood smoke. Lorain and several of the grandchildren were off cooking the rest in the biggest stew pot anyone could imagine.

Standing guard over the smoker for the next three days was going to have to be a shared task around the compound. Everyone made Rudy take the first 8-hour shift because he shot the damn thing; three days later the meat was ready. Blake and Lorain had rigged up some old vacuum pumps they got from an automotive garage to help preserve the meat. Normally, during canning season, it would get processed along with the crops, but smoking and vacuum packing would have to be done for now.

Edina Iowa: An aging, worn out Big Al was lounging around in a small, deserted house just north of the Fabius

River. He had landed here after walking for nearly 9 months, a year or so back. He figured he was finally far enough away from all his enemies, the ones he knew about and the ones he did not. He spent most days fishing the banks and drinking tea he made from some plant that grew next to the water. He had no idea what it was, but he chewed a piece out of boredom one day and it had a nice taste and seemed to relax him. For all he knew, it could have been marijuana, wild hemp, or something poisonous, he did not care, he just liked it. The small town to the south had about 20 people living there, and they all seemed to be normal, or at least apocalyptic normal. Al did not want to fight any more battles; he wanted no bikers chasing him, and definitely no more bears. That last one he battled almost killed him. Never in his life did he ever think he would have to kill a bear with a damn machete. But the stubborn animal tasted good.

Al often wondered where his friends Blake and Lorain were. And what about their sons and all of Lorain's family? Someday, when life was nearly gone, he wanted to return to his small house over in Illinois and lay his head down one more time.

The Compound: It is now day 3,750 and everything seems to run as smoothly as expected. Blake and Lorain had recently put the last of their two dogs, Mandy and Sam, to rest. It would be an adjures job, but new dogs would have to be found. Loading up the MRAP, the two had decided to head west to the Iron Rock trading post. Nearly 150 miles away, it was a trip that they did not make often. After mixing additives into a 50-gallon drum of diesel, the large truck was ready to roll. Pulling Blake's old 14-foot trailer full of stuff to trade, they headed out.

When the couple reached the trading post, they were amazed, it looked like an old-time county fair. Everything imaginable was there for trade. Blake, un-tarped his goods and began to set up a makeshift stand. The harvest from last season was massive. More vegetables than the people in the compound could eat in three years. Piles of jars, packs of smoked meat, and scavenged tools were just some of his goodies. Lorain, on the other hand, slipped into her combat gear, grabbed her AR15 and began to patrol.

Something changed in Lorain with that big supply-run down south. Mowing down a dozen people with a full-sized garbage truck might have been a bit much. She was the greatest grandma ever, but you did not want to cross her.

A time after the supply-run, I am not sure what the date was, but some scavengers, the 2-legged kind, were raiding the compounds supplies. No one even noticed but Lorain. She adorned herself up with camo face paint and a full loadout of gear then disappeared into the forest one night after dark. Blake protested and said he would go, but she cut him off and simply said; "I need to do this". When she returned about 30 hours later, she was covered in dirt and blood. She just stared out into the woods for an entire day after that. Blake finally poked her enough to get her mad. She screamed; "THEY ARE NOT COMING BACK!" "THEY WILL NEVER BOTHER ANYONE AGAIN!"

After that, Lorain would not even sleep without her short barreled AR15, and her small Glock 42 tucked beneath her pillow. It took weeks before she would even let her own husband near her again.

The east woods, sometime earlier: "Shhhh, they will hear us." Expressed Grunge, as he laid in the field just east of the compound. Bobby whispered back, "Who, the old dude or the old bitch? They can't hear us you dumb ass... We need to get to that field behind that trailer, I swear that is where they keep the good shit." Grunge looked at Bobby, he rolled his eyes and said, "The tomatoes and cabbage we got yesterday was good, but I want their stash of meat. It has to be back there somewhere; let's go." Sneaking along the east side of the compound, the two came upon what looked like the end of a small road. A cabin was to the right and an overgrown field lay in the northwest. A large pile of trees lay in a strange looking pile. It kind of looked like a barricade of brush. The two ran across the small road and sprinted towards the pile. Once they were there, they poked around to find it was on wheels. It was piled on an old 15-foot trailer that could be swung or pulled out of the way. Scrambling to the ground and crawling under the front of the pile, Grunge whispered, "Look, a meat smoker, and check out all that dried meat hanging in those bags. There must be 50 pounds of it."

As they snuck across the small, graveled hidden space, they grabbed everything they could. Grunge grabbed bags of meat while Bobby grabbed a basket of fresh garden vegetables. Running with their arms full, the two sprinted for the far backside of the property. They had a great haul, and they were going to enjoy it.

Lorain lay in the weeds just 30 feet from the fire, she listened to the two yammer on about all the women they ever had and all the ones they would have once they took all the food from this place. Thinking she would just pop up and shoot the two gave her a pause. She had not seen any guns yet, but if they had them, at best she may be able to kill one and wound another before she was shot herself. She had to lure them away from their camp. She was no spring chicken, but she was built. She was stronger and faster than most men she knew, even her sweet husband Blake. She had an idea.

Sitting around a small fire, chewing their spoils, Grunge and Bobby heard something. As Grunge reached for his knife, a nearly naked Lorain appeared from the woods and said, "What's up boys? Is that all the meat you want?" She gave them a wicked smile and winked. Lorain took off in a dead run, as she tore through the woods back to her clothes, pack and weapons, the two chased and screamed. "Hey old lady, wait on us, we want to party, we don't want to hurt you, we just want to fuck your dead corpse. Here kitty kitty…"

Lorain knew she had messed up; she was sure the two would just follow her to their deaths, now she was thinking it would be hers. As she threw on her pants and a shirt, she felt her body get slammed from the side. She grappled with the smaller Bobby on the ground; she twisted her body and pulled his arm up between her massive legs and twisted again. SNAP went the arm of the dirty little bastard. Spinning around, she saw the larger one, Grunge, as he came crashing through the trees. Lorain picked up her pack and swung the entire thing like a bat. Whoosh, it hit the man in full run and sent him headfirst into an old stump. The rotten stump exploded from the impact, and he hollered and rolled sideways. As Lorain scrambled for her gun, Grunge grabbed her ankle and pulled. Reaching under her bra, she grabbed the small knife Blake always forced her to carry. She lashed out screaming like a mad woman catching Grunge in the forearm. As he pulled back, Lorain rose to her feet, the scariest looking woman anyone had ever seen. Blood dripping from her knife and her face, she lunged, she stabbed and sliced and stabbed until Grunge moved no more. She turned to Bobby and sprang like a cat. She screamed, "STEAL MY GRANDCHILDRENS FOOD WILL YOU…! NO, NO, YOU WILL NOT, YOU SCREWED WITH THE WRONG GRANDMA."

The Compound: Three days after heading for the trading post, the large lumbering truck with two German Shepard puppies in it rolled back into the compound. Actually, they were part Shepard and part Malinois. The two had never trained dogs before, but they did stay in a Holiday Inn Express one time, ha ha ha, a joke for the old-timers, so they were good. The two dogs, Specter and Shrek, would be their new best friends. The names were picked from an old Zombie, end of the world, book Blake had read many years before.

Blake and Lorain, acting like teenagers most of the time, were happy. They had planned for this and survived. They had their offspring living with them and they were all healthy. The ghosts of the past would visit them in their dreams from time to time, but they mostly would stay quiet, at least for a few more years. The children would grow.

They would have babies, they would grow, and the cycle of life would continue in the great north on the "Grid Down Compound."

Chapter 14 – The ANG

The Compound: Word had got to the compound, after a long period of Blake transmitting with never a reply, that the old Army National Guard, now just known as the ANG, was completely rogue and hunting anyone who challenged them. The Madison Enclave, that the compound residents were so careful to stay away from, was rumored to be their stronghold. And the ANG was headed north.

The compound's security was not as strong as it needed to be for this new type of threat. Blake, Lorain, Zed, Rudy, Shauna, and Maya were the core of the compound's security. John and Rachel, being only 18 and 15, were already well trained at long distance shooting but could not go toe-to-toe with an attacking force. At best, they could lay down cover fire and provide general overwatch.

Zed and Rudy had been scavenging north up towards the old college town with a lot of success lately, they had brought back trailer loads of supplies. The only way these trips were possible was to use some high-end ATVs and UTVs that were capable of multifuel operation. A large barn, behind what looked like a million-dollar house, is where these were found. Sometimes you just had to love those rich bastards. For these to work, a large supply of propane had to be located. Tanks were taken from every camper and garage in the area. Since most were half empty, they were topped off at the old methane liquification plant. Now this mixture burned like hell fire and was as dangerous as hell itself, but it worked. It even worked on the multi fuel generators.

Some of those scavenging missions returned hundreds of pounds of dynamite from some of the old copper mines and a bunch of Tannerite from Wolly World and Dundee's Sporting goods. Now Tannerite would not be very useful by itself, but mixed and packed tight around a stick of leaky dynamite made a really dangerous weapon. Tape that to a methane canister and you could blow a 20-foot-wide and 20-foot-deep hole in the ground. For a last resort, they could blow the bridge 10 miles down on 45 to isolate themselves. But that would only be in a dire emergency.

When the boys first showed up with this stuff, Blake was furious. He could not figure out why they would bring this overly dangerous shit back to the compound, there was no way this stuff could stay. Since it was already there, he had the boys store it in the old Barker farm outbuildings. One of the things the boys did not tell him about was the 80 bags of ammonium nitrate fertilizer that was in the same buildings. Seeming like the plot of a really bad movie, the farm had enough explosives or explosive making materials to remove everything for three miles in every direction. Hell, if they mixed the tractor hydraulic fluid stored on the farm with that fertilizer, you could just kiss everything goodbye.

When everyone got together to discuss the situation, the boys finally fessed up to everything they had stashed at the Barkers. They even let out a bit more secret. They had hit every gun store, house, and police department for a 75-mile radius. They had even found a military munitions armory in the warehouse district over in L'Anse. The Barker house had become a secret armory. Blake, being a bit grouchy when he was left out of the loop, stood up and walked over to the boys and just stared at them. Five minutes passed and he said, "Good fucking job, I am proud of you two."

After the meeting, it was decided that Lorain and Shauna, who strangely enough did not always see eye to eye, would head west to Iron Rock to look for help. If they could find 10 to 20 people to fight with them, they could keep the soon to be invaders at bay. The dangerous part would be the 15-mile trip south before they could head west. The two fueled up their methane powered ATV's and got ready to set out. Blake came bounding around from the shop with two of his hush mufflers he made. All the UTVs were modified to take one. It made it virtually impossible to hear them. Rolling her eyes as he attached them, Lorain could only think, "Here comes the Clampetts."

Once the two got close to Bob's crossing, nothing looked right. The normally deserted town was no longer overgrown with weeds; they were all flattened. The two quickly ditched their ATVs and headed into the brush along the old road. Sneaking along behind the old campground, they quickly saw what they did not want to. The ANG was not in Madison, it was here. About 300 of them. Damn, they would never make it to get help. Their entire encampment was completely on the east side of 45 taking up about a solid mile of Route 28. This gave the two an idea, but they had to make it back home first. As they crawled back through the buildings and overgrown bushes, they heard something. A young girl was on her knees before a large man with his pants down. Before either could do a thing, the man pulled back from her and blew her head into a mist with a short, barreled shotgun. The fat man mumbled as he pulled up his pants, "Bitch, I told you, NO TEETH!"

ANG Campsite, Route 45: Colonel Randal Foster could not believe he was sent back to this wasteland. The wasn't any dissidents up here, just psychopaths that should have died a long time ago. They had just wiped out a group of about 30 cannibals the day before. Fifty miles south of where they were camped at Bob's crossing was a nightmare like no other. They had found bones from dozens of cooked and eaten people. He thought that if he did find who they sent him up here to look for, he would kill them all. There would never be a reason for him to come back to this hell.

Boom… A gun blast went off somewhere to the right of the Colonel. "Dammit, what the hell is going on now? We have got to get the hell out of here." he thought.

The Compound: Back at the compound, the girls returned with sour faces; they could barely get the story from their mouths. They would have to come up with a plan; these fuckers could not be left alive to treat people this way. After Blake had listened for a bit, he had heard all he needed to. No one would be spared, they all needed to die. The group needed to keep the ANG where they were and take them out in place. The location of the compound had to stay a secret. To keep the compound from being discovered, as it almost was, the last time the ANG came through, both ends of the road had been blocked. Thousands of piled up trees from the wood yard four miles to the west were toppled over to block that end. Trees were cut down and dropped over all the other roads that headed south. You had to head south, west, north, east, then south again to leave the area. The complex blocked roads mostly kept the curious away. The residents of the compound used the old ATV trails for actual travel.

The general plan was to get one of the garbage trucks running again and use it for a massive explosive truck bomb. Rudy was the lucky person to head to the dump and try to find Bernie and get one of the trucks. After loading his pack and grabbing his rifle, he began the five-mile walk through the woods. Popping out at the truck lot, Rudy dropped to the ground as a shot rang out. Rudy screamed, "Dammit Bernie, stop shooting at me!" Bernie just hollered back, "You better of brought me some chocolate or you are a dead man." Rudy popped up and walked towards him and handed over the last of the hotel chocolates. Once Bernie got done cussing, about these being the same ones he got before, he asked what he was there for.

A few hours later, one of the big trucks roared to life. Rudy asked how Bernie still had functioning batteries. Bernie just laughed and said, "I drain them, then I refill and charge one whenever I need one. Boy, how stupid are you?" Rudy, rolling his eyes just smiled and thought, "This guy is worse

than dealing with Dad. Dad is not nearly as fucking crazy."
He turned and hopped up in the truck and started the 10-
mile complex twisting and turning drive back to the
compound.

Now Blake, being a former IT guy, had researched and
documented everything that normal people should not. He
dug way back in a corner of the communications bunker
and brought out one of his, how-to, binders labeled
explosives. Handing it off to Maya, he just told her to start
reading. Two hours later, the boys were measuring precise
amounts of hydraulic oil and mixing it into the 80 bags of
fertilizer. The bags were mixed and carefully placed inside
the garbage truck with 10 canisters of Methane, 330 pounds
of dynamite, and 200 pounds of mixed Tannerite. The idea
was to trigger the explosion by squeezing the total contents
with the 20 thousand pounds of hydraulic pressure that the
trash compactor could produce. Just deciding who would
set it off was not going to be easy.

Blake, being the leader of the group, was not going to let
any of his family deliver this device. He would do it
himself. Blake wanted one more item to go along with the
truck; one of those 1000-gallon methane trailers like they
pulled when they went on that supply run some years back.
After a long goodbye and Blake reassuring everyone that
he had a plan and would be long gone and back at the
compound by the time it went off, he pulled out from the
old Barker farm. Winding his way around up north to head
back south, Blake had to slam the brakes on the lumbering
beast. Damn Bernie was sitting in the road on that stupid

lawn chair again. Blake hollered, "Bernie, you dumb ass, I was just coming to see you. I need that 1000-gallon tank trailer again." Bernie just laughed and tilted his head as he said, "You dummy, you had a 200-gallon last time, the 1000 is huge, is that really what you want?" Smiling and thinking to himself, hell yes, that will definitely do it.

Two hours later the trailer was attached and packed to its maximum pressure. Blake attached his last home-made detonator directly to the top. When the big one goes, this one will cause a fireball that will incinerate everything for a mile. That was the last thought Blake had before a sharp pain in his head forced everything to go dark.

Bernie stood over Blake's limp body and checked to make sure he was still breathing. "Sorry my friend, you have a family, and I have nothing left." Now Bernie had lost more than anyone would ever know. Even though he lived and worked at the dump for years, he had a family, they just did not want anything to do with him. His family had survived the crash but did not survive some raiders in their small town on the Wisconsin and Illinois border. As far as Bernie was concerned, the ANG that Rudy had told him about were as good as any for his revenge. They even could have been the ones that killed them.

Revving the engine on the massive truck, Bernie shifted it into first and it rolled to life. Winding his way west around all the blocked roads, Bernie turned left onto old Route 45 and floored the big truck. Bernie figured if they were on their way up and not still at Bob's crossing he could mow them down at this rate of speed. If they were not, his biggest worry would be them hearing him as he tried to make the hard left onto Route 28. As he traveled along, he reflected on a life formerly lost. His young daughter Bethany and his wife June used to live here with him. June had divorced him when he refused to quit his job at the dump. Their little house was stuffed with crap that he always brought home. The last he had heard of them was when her sister Barb came through not long after the crash and told him of the deaths. Bernie went a bit insane after that, he had moved into the dump and proclaimed it as his kingdom.

Thirty minutes later he was woken from his daydream by his windshield splintering across his view. He swerved slightly and lowered himself down to avoid getting shot. Not seeing anyone, he figured these were just advanced guards or scouts. He pushed the pedal to the floor and roared down the road. Breaking as carefully as he could he began to veer left through the old gas station, running down pumps and anything else that was there. As he did this the bullets began to pepper the truck from every angle. As far as he could tell, he had made it to the center of their encampment. Slamming on the brakes, he got the lumbering beast to stop. He slid down onto the floor and slapped the garbage compactor switch and screamed, "YOU WILL ALL PAY FOR MY DAUGHTER! DIE FUCKERS DIE!"

The Colonel was busy taking a nap after some amorous activity with his First Sergeant. She hated his stinking ass, but it kept her on light duty and eating the best foods. As he sprang to his feet, he yelled, "That's the northern scouts, get someone up there." Before he could even finish his order, he saw the truck. It had already made it to the center of their encampment. Bullets were riddling the truck when he heard something that sounded like a crunching sound. The last thought that went through his head was, "Really! you're dumping your garbage here?"

Back at the compound the explosion shook the ground like nothing they had felt since the grid had failed. Lorain ran from the bunker and screamed, "Blake, Blake, you asshole, what did you do?" A silence fell over the compound as Blake stumbled from the woods, bleeding from his head, and collapsed onto the field. Hovering over an unconscious Blake, Lorain sobbed, she whispered to him, "You dumb English Bull Dog, it is a good thing I like you." Several seconds later, a groggy Blake muttered, "I have not heard you say that since before the crash. It's a good thing I like you to." Jumping from her seat she screamed out the door, "He's awake, He's awake." Sitting up in his bed with his family encircling him he tried to make a joke, "If this was an action movie, It would have taken five blows to the head and 10 gunshots to take me down." Everyone laughed at one more of dad's stupid jokes.

For the next few days, everyone was still tense, Rudy wanted to travel down to the blast site and finish off anyone left. The group overruled that idea, and they decided to keep all the blinds in place and place an extra guard down in the woodyard. After the three of them took turns on overwatch for the next week, they decided they were finally safe.

Chapter 15 – The Compound

Life around the compound went on. Scavenging supplies, having babies, and just life in general was always happening. The group was hard and soft at the same time. They competed for everything they did; someone was always trying to outdo someone.

Maya and Shauna had been busier than anyone. They seemed to be competing for mom of the decade. They both have had three children by this point. Maya had three dark haired beautiful girls, and Shauna had three rough and tumbling boys. If anyone really knew the truth, those girls were way tougher than those boys could ever dream of.

The dirty duo, as they called themselves. John and Rachel were a force to be reckoned with. After watching their father bleed out on the floor and not knowing what happened to their mother, the two were hard. They outworked everyone every day and spent every evening with their Grandma Lorain. She was more of a mom to them than anyone would know and the two would obliterate anyone or thing that would threaten her. Her only rival might have been Grandpa Blake.

Zed and Rudy were the kings of bringing unique stuff back. ATVs, UTVs, Motorcycles, and some things that no one knew what to do with. Blake had picked out a couple of these that he would keep and work on. All the functional vehicles for at least ten miles in each direction had been rounded up and brought back to the compound.

It was not beyond Blake's capabilities to go on some private scavenging missions all his own though. The boys were great, but they were all brute force and no finesse. Blake would disappear into the woods like a chameleon, camouflaged from head to toe and carrying a full combat load of gear, he would sometimes be gone for a week at a time. This always worried Lorain, she just knew she would have to go rescue him someday with her brute force approach. She would go in like an Army division and blow everything away first and then see what was left.

A few years after the ANG was blown to pieces, down at Bob's Crossing, the traffic through the area began to pick back up. The occasional passer-through became more frequent. People who had fled from the Russians, so many years back, were making the trip back east more and more. In order to keep these travelers out of the fields, the blocks at both ends of the road were not removed but rearranged. You could now pass with a single six-foot-wide cart or motorized vehicle if you were so fortunate to have one.

On one particular day, the travelers seemed to be higher in numbers than they had ever seen. A few of them strayed into the compound searching for whatever. When the alarms sounded and the boy's road up on their Mad Max ATVs, the group dropped to the ground and began to shake and scream. The screaming from them and the ones on the roads was soon at a deafening pitch. "Don't shoot, don't shoot, we are not runaways, please don't send us back." Blake hopped down from the southern lookout post and walked over. He stood looking at these refugees and asked, "What are you doing here? You should know to stick to the roads; everyone knows to STICK to the road." One skinny little man replied, "We don't mister, we are not from here, we have traveled for days and have no idea where we are. If you are with them, please don't send us back! We just thought we could find supplies in that old camper in the field."

Blake was a bit frustrated; the damn camper had the camouflaged blind removed again. Lorain knew better but she was airing everything out for the season. Someday, they would pull that old thing out of there, but it was their first "home" they had on the land. Keeping it was a bit sentimental.

Looking down at the shaking guy he was talking to; Blake smiled and said, "We're sorry we scared you... I do not know who you are talking about, and it doesn't sound like I want to. My sons will take you down the road and show you how to get out of this area. There is a road not too far that will take you east. That area is mostly uninhabited; you should be safe there."

Four hours later, the boys returned with the details of where they took them. They were taken down passed the old spring and were allowed to fill up on as much water as they could carry, then taken north until they hit old Route 38.

That would take them to the lake, then they can continue from there.

Blake was concerned, he had not heard of any group close to them that was oppressing its masses. Maybe they just stayed isolated too much. He knew of the Madison Enclave and heard about some violence over in Minnesota, but that was about it. No one from the Chicago area even came up in this direction anymore. After blowing the ANG to hell, no one from anywhere south came up this way.

Iron Rock, seventy miles to the east: Frank, "The Wraith," Slone, was sipping a cup of coffee laced with the finest single malt bourbon he could find. It really wasn't his, but the dead guy he took it from would not miss it. Frank had traveled almost 800 miles to get where he was. After losing his entire gang along with all his family to some punk in a fancy UTV, and getting shot in the head to boot, he just headed north. It would not be the first time he had relocated. Originally from the deserts of Arizona, he would move when he could no longer control an area. He would recruit a new gang and take over a new town. After all, the world had ended, he was still here. By God's own hand, he was supposed to be king. He commonly considered himself the new Messiah. The people of Iron Rock would worship him or die.

Southern Illinois, seventeen days after the collapse: Frank was traveling north, and he was picking up all kinds of strays. Down around the southern tip of Illinois, there had been a massive earthquake and some kind of massive explosion. He did not know what happened, but burned, dying people were everywhere. It was there that God told him he was to survive and rule. He had camped out next to a large crevice that looked to be bigger than the Grand Canyon nursing his gaping head wound for about a week. It was then that he started to get the daily headaches. His entire head would throb, and when they were at their worst, he would here from God. "You are my seventh son; you have proved yourself to me. Gather my flock, travel to the northern promised lands, and rule as I would!"

Moving north slowly in or on any type of vehicle he could find, he gathered followers. Hell had come to these parts; anyone who survived would follow him or die. All hail The Wraith. For about nine years, Frank stopped and terrorized any small community he could find. He would kill, maim, and rape until they could give no more. His followers were even more brutal than him. They would stick out the winters wherever they were, feeding on the citizens in more than just one way. If the towns could not supply him with his favorite meal, a bowl of peppermint ice cream, he would feast on their flesh instead. Eating the flesh of all the creatures is what God instructed him to do. He would consume their souls, and his power would increase.

The Compound: Blake had decided that he and Zed were going on an information run. They would never head south if it could be avoided, but Route 28 was the only way east and it all intersected at Bob's Crossing. They could go farther south to Watersmeet but that might be even more dangerous. That is where Blake and Lorain got ambushed by the crazies so many years back.

Blake had returned from one of his personal scavenging missions with some military-looking desert vehicle. It ran on diesel like fuel and was pretty stout. Blake never told the boys where he got it or much about it, it was his little secret. This would be the fastest way down southwest to look around.

Loaded for combat, the two took off at about 5AM the next morning. They hoped the ride would be fast and uneventful. Tooling down Route 45 they immediately got a wake-up call; at the bottom of the gorge sat what looked like an old school bus... It was so dirty; you could barely see the old yellow paint. Stopping to check it out and clear the area, the two bounded towards the abandoned bus, at least they hoped it was abandoned. Closer and closer they eventually saw what looked like a body slumping over the steering wheel. It definitely was a body, and it was definitely dead. Climbing inside, they almost tossed up their breakfast. Chains and restraints were adorned on every seat. The smell of death and excrement burned their noses. Zed looked at Blake and asked, "Do you think those refugees were on this? They did not mention it, but if you remember how weak they looked, this makes sense. No way could they have walked very far. When we got to the spring, they drank like they never seen water before."

After checking all around, the two decided they could not leave this thing here. If they could get it rolling towards the old roadside stop, they could maybe get it into the river. The river was not up currently, but next thaw it would whisk the thing away. A lot of pushing and pulling with dads' new toy and they had it lined up for a straight downhill run into the river. Zed looked at his dad and asked, "What is this thing, it looks like a UTV but has the power of a bulldozer." Blake just smiled and grabbed the big rock from under the bus tire. The bus took off like a shot. Down the hill and just barely made the small drive into the rest area. It launched off the old bridge pier next to the river and landed in a crash. Hoping that if anyone came to find it, they would not look just around the bend of the river.

Moving on, they had made it down to Bob's Crossing and had to stop in amazement. The entire east side of the small town was gone. A crater 50 feet wide and 30 feet deep was all that was left. Piles of blown down and burned old buildings were everywhere. What looked like dehydrated body parts were scattered amongst it. No one from the group was allowed down here since Bernie blew the shit out of the area, and this was why.

On instinct, Blake said they could not head towards Iron Rock. He wanted to go south until they met Route 2 before they turned. Zed just looked at him and shrugged his shoulders. Hammering the throttle, the buggy rocketed out the south side of town. Since the tree line was always cut way back up here, the road was still pretty passable. So, Blake kept the speed up to about 60. They reached Watersmeet less than an hour later. The town was not big, but it did have one of the biggest ATV dealers in the area. Pulling into the lot, they just sat and looked for a while. Blake: "Do you see anything moving?" Zed: "No, it looks deserted."

After 20 minutes, the two snuck to the side of the old dealership. Pushing open a window to peer inside, they saw a horrifying site. Human bodies were gutted like animals and hanging from the ceiling. The place had been turned into a human meat locker. Gagging and barely able to breathe, the two ran for the UTV and jumped in. Just about then, rocks, sticks, and pieces of debris came flying their way. A mob of what used to be humans were running directly at them. Barely intelligible screaming came from the group. "Get away from our food!", "We found it first!" "God will judge you for your trespass!" A quick decision had to be made, grabbing both of their M4's with 200 round drums attached, they staggered fully automatic bursts of fire at the group. Each would fire off a burst of about ten and yell, "Fire!" "Set!" "Fire!"

They went back and forth like this through at least 150 rounds each. When they stopped, piles of bullet riddled bodies laid before them. They were adorned in rags and skins that neither wanted to speculate where they came from.

Bending over to vomit, Zed heaved until there was nothing left. He looked at his father and asked, "Why did we come here? You were adamant on coming this direction." Blake just turned and replied, "I have no idea, we just needed to.

Maybe we were here to right an evil. If that is so, I think we just did."

Grabbing two Gerry cans from the UTV, they began to cover all the bodies in fuel. The stuff was a homemade mixture Blake had come up with, and he was not sure it would burn, but it was worth a try. To his surprise, it burned just like diesel fuel. Hard to start but impossible to put out. Zed pulled down the last can and held it up for Blake to see, without a word, he pointed at the meat market. No words passed after that; all the fires were lit and the two headed west on old Route 2.

Keeping totally silent and cruising about 35 miles an hour, the two were probably in shock and did not even know it. A couple of hours later they saw where Routes 2 and 28 came together. A large barricade had been erected, just 1000 feet beyond the intersection. The last time they were down here for trading, no such thing existed. This was new, and it was large. A voice called out, "Trading or passing through?" If your trading, it better be good, if you are passing through, we will just take what you have anyways." Looking around for a quick way out, Blake noticed several small roads that disappeared into an old burned-out neighborhood. He could floor it and make the hard right easy enough. Thinking twice, he just started making stuff up, in his best English accent, he spoke. "I am Sir Lawrance Masterson, emissary of King Brown, the ruler of the Madison Enclave. We bring a request for trade between our communities. We will trade goods and supplies for smoked meats of any kind."

Laughter rang out and three large men revealed themselves. "Smoked meat, you say, what if we turn you into smoked meat? After all, you are coming from our hunting grounds." Zed raised two Glock 18 fully automatic pistols and sprayed 30 rounds at the crew in less than 10 seconds. The fight did not even get a chance to start. The three were dead before they even fell to the ground. Blake turned and shook his head, "That was a lot of ammo for just three guys, what are we going to do now? We certainly can't ask them any questions." Looking around, Zed shrugged his shoulders, smiled and said, "It was better than listening to anymore of that horrible accent you were trying to do. Any more I would have had to shoot you too."

Looking around the small town, it would not be easy to search, if anyone was there and heard the shots, it would be downright impossible. The statement the three made about cooking and smoking the two of them and that they had come from the hunting grounds was a bit disturbing. Had cannibalism spread everywhere?

Carefully driving around, the town and the lake, the two finally saw what they wanted. It had to be where the men from the blockade were staying. A small house with just a whiff of smoke coming from the chimney. Doing their best imitation of two cops in an action-packed drama, they entered and cleared the house. "Clear", "Clear over here to." What they found disturbed them even more. A map of the entire area was laid on a large table. The markings all over the map made it easy to figure out. It was sectioned off about every 10 square miles with a different color and lines or x's. Iron Rock was labeled as, "The Holy Land". Where they just came from was labeled, "The Feed Lot." Way down by Rhinelander was labeled, "COVID Dead Zone." And the most disturbing was the block around their area; "The Devils Hideout – Needs Cleansed".

Racing up Route 28 as fast as they could push the UTV, Blake and Zed, with all the information they had gathered, they only wanted to get home. They would have to blow that bridge.

Chapter 16 – The Cleanse

Iron Rock: The Wraith stood up on his motorcycle, holding a long metal rod with 3 heads hanging from it. He screamed, "These three non-believers were killed because their faith in me was not true. They let the east side of the Holy Land be desecrated by the devil's seven minions. We will kill, cook, and eat the souls of our enemies. No one challenges my rule. God himself now fears me!" The engines screamed, the tires smoked, and the search for the seven spawns of the devil began.

The Compound: Blake and Zed just pulled onto the compound when the big UTV sputtered and died. The fuel was gone, and they had burned the rest destroying the bodies. Blake ran to the backside of the trailer and spun the old antique air raid siren. It was a bit loud, but it would pull in everyone. Waiting in the field for everyone to show up, Blake tried to process what they had just experienced. Zed hopped on one of the propane/methane powered ATV's and headed to the old Barker house where their auxiliary armory was. He pulled the largest cart the ATV could pull; he would return with it loaded to capacity.

As all the compound dwellers descended onto the field carrying their firearms and gear, Blake's face told of something being wrong. He said in the calmest voice he could muster, "We will be protecting or blowing the gorge bridge within an hour, depending on who gets there first. Maya, get all the kids in the new bunker. It has everything you will need for two months. If one of us don't come to get you within 24 hours, we are all dead." Maya just stared back at him and nodded. Blake spoke again, "The other seven of us fight, even John and Rachel. Zed will be back with explosives and more gear in a few minutes; everyone go get your ATVs. Full battle rattle is required, GO NOW, you have 20 minutes."

As the four raced off, Zed pulled back into the compound with more gear than they could use. He quickly dumped about two-thirds onto the field. Pointing to the rest, he said, "I'm leaving this down at the start of the 45-south turn. It will be just inside the trees. If we must retreat, I want some arms waiting on us. I'm heading there now. Then I will be down there at the bridge setting the explosives." Zed then fired up his ATV "Mad Max" and headed out.

Once everyone returned, Blake started to hand out the arms and give directions. Blake: "Everyone will carry four firearms. John and Rachel will be on high overwatch and sniping duty. You two will carry your 308, a fully auto M4, a Glock 18 clone, and your personal backup weapon. Everyone else grab the same except replace the 308 with a 30 round, drum fed, autoloading shotgun. We pull out in 10." A short time later they all were rocketing towards the unknown.

As Blake reached the intersection of 26 and 45, where 45 heads south, he paused and thought, "Damn, what if they took the long way around, the way through the small town of Silver City would take longer but the area is almost completely deserted." That area was always sparse for people except during skiing season. Deciding to play it safe, Blake asked Shauna to rocket up towards the next town, Rockland, and keep a lookout from high up on the cell tower. He told her to fire off six shotgun blasts into the air and hit her transmit key six times if she sees anyone coming through the valley. Now a person short, they continued to the river.

Frank Slone sat at the crossroads of old 28 and forest road 64 and thought. He was absolutely mad, but he was not stupid. He had survived his dad, the asshole in the Smokies, a gunshot to the head and even camping inside a nuclear waste zone. That massive demon that beat seven of his followers to death had to be the spawn of satin himself. He would need to survive fighting this devil as well. Standing up on his pegs, he yelled, "We head north, we will sneak up on the devil from his back door and that will be our salvation. We are in his domain; kill everyone you see along the way." Revving the massive bike, he rocketed north with his 43 holy warriors on his tail.

Back at the river gorge, Blake was starting to worry, they should have already been here, if they were coming at all. Even if they walked, they should have been here by now. With sweat on his brow, he started to panic. He rousted everyone from their dug-in positions and screamed for them to get back up the hill. The attack was coming from Silver City, not Bob's crossing. Zed grabbed some ice fishing line and quickly ran trip lines across four locations across the bridge. If Blake was wrong, the bridge would blow and stop the southern attack.

Near the top of the cell tower, Shauna saw it coming, it looked like a wave slowly washing up the road. She pointed her shotgun back towards the southern defenses and let off six blasts and keyed her radio the same. She could only hope they were herd. Blake was hammering his ATV so hard trying to get to the top of the east side of the valley, he did not hear a thing. Ten minutes later as he slowed to a craw, he saw it, Shauna was hauling ass straight towards him. "Oh shit, she saw something", and he missed the signal.

The Stormm's all stopped in the road and waited. Shauna came rolling up and told them the force of people was about 40 strong and on a multitude of different motorcycles and such. There was a group of about 10 that were outpacing the rest and would arrive a full five minutes earlier. The plan quickly evolved to be the same as before. Another smaller river lay just behind them. It had a wicked bridge on a blind curve. If they could trap them there, they could survive this. Zed took off on his ATV and headed for the bridge. He had just enough explosives left to do something with. Looking at the bridge and then the rockface at their end, he had a new plan. Zed began packing the explosives inside a large fisher at the base of the small cliff. He screamed behind him as the others sought covered firing positions, "If they make it this far, I will blow the cliff, it should crush everything and collapse the bridge."

Blake positioned four people at the edge of the bridge closest to the coming horde. He explained, "I want an M4, running full auto, on each side, aimed at a 45-degree angle from the road, this will keep you from shooting each other. Shauna and Rudy, these are your posts. Five yards from each will be Lorain and I, we will unload our 30 round shotgun drums on them. When everyone runs dry, reverse the roles. That means we will have unleashed a full 120 rounds at them. While we all reload, Zed will open up with big Bertha from smack dab in the middle of the road. Rachel and John will drop anyone left standing. I want the M4's on 3-round burst after that. We want them to think we are a force from Hell." Zed proceeded to hoist his Browning 30 caliber monster up to the front of his massive ATV, Mad Max. This collector's piece had not been fired for years, but its former owner had restored it to mint condition. Storing the 20, full boxes, of belt fed ammo was a bit excessive, but greatly appreciated.

As Frank Slone, The Wraith, rounded the corner before the bridge he slowed just a bit, he was so far out in front of everyone, he was vulnerable. Deciding to just pull over and let the entire group catch up may have been the best or worst thing he had done. Once all the slower, motorcycles, ATVs, and two damn mopeds, caught up, he gave one more pep talk. "We are close, once we get out of this ravine, we will be in hell's back yard. All of you will reign in my kingdom for this noble act." The motors roared and his followers screamed. "Kill! Kill! Kill!"

The large group approached, running no more than ten miles per hour, the Stormm's readied themselves. The M4's spit fire and the shotguns roared like thunder. The lead bike swerved and careened off the road. Frank tried to keep control but found himself flying over the handlebars and landing with a thud. The next few bikes got tangled with each other and the entire hoard smashed directly into them. People were scrambling to get off and run but were quickly cut down. The M4's and the shotguns had run dry. The hoard had turned into a mangled mass of bodies and twisted steel in less than 60 seconds.

The roar, the smoke, and the screaming were not like in the movies. Everyone was temporarily blind and deaf from the hundreds of continuous explosions. Blake thought to himself, "Welcome to Hell." Blake looked towards Zed and screamed, "NOW!" Zed opened up and Hell exploded. His rounds ripped through everything. Pink mist filled the air and covered everyone south of the road. When the massive gun silenced, Grambo, aka Lorain, was up on the road sinking rounds into every moving body. She was doing her "protect the family" thing again. This must have been what it was like when she hunted down those thieves some years back. Blake yelled for everyone to retreat towards Zed's location as fast as their legs would carry them. Once they were all assembled, Blake, with fire in his eyes screamed at Zed, "BLOW THE FUCKING CLIFF!" Zed leveled his rifle at his Tannerite detonator and fired. As the 5.56 round screamed to the target at over 3000 feet per second, the reactive target material exploded and set off their last 40 pounds of dynamite. The sound and the percussions were massive, the shockwave threw the group backwards as the cliff, the bridge, and the pile of bodies and bikes all disappeared.

Lying at the bottom of the small ravine, Frank looked at his broken body and thought, "God has forsaken me; he did not respect my power. When I return from hell, even heaven will pay." As he lay there, the last large boulder began to work loose from the cliff. It rolled and bounced, and acting as the finger of God, it smashed to the bottom where Frank was reduced to a pile of red goo.

As the Stormm's finished mopping up, Shauna passed out from exhaustion. Rudy ran to her side and laid her head on his lap to slowly give her water. The rest of the Stormm's were experiencing mild shock symptoms as the adrenaline left their bodies. Everyone sat on the road looking at each other, most were covered in blood and gore. No one had imagined how blood spray in the air would travel. After 20 more minutes, Zed spoke, "Our work is done here, we need to head back and check the north road into the area. If that looks clear, we can go home." Looking at his blood splattered boots, Blake shook his head and confirmed. "He is right, there is one more road we need to check, let's go."

Chapter 17 – Going Home

It has been twenty years since the collapse of the grid. Rudy, Shauna, Zed, and Maya's families have grown. A total of eleven Stormm grandchildren and three great grandchildren now live on, and maintain, about 1,000 acres in the great north. The wilderness has pretty much taken back everything that surrounds the expanded Grid Down Compound. Some old neighbors had returned over the years but never seemed to stay. The cold winters were too much without the modern comforts of the past. And of course, the ever-looming threat of the next group of crazed or power-hungry psychopaths coming to conquer the area was always on their minds.

Blake and Lorain, being 75 and 80, desired to make the trek south one more time before they passed. Both, being extremely fit for their age, seemed to be more like they were in their sixties than their actual age. Drawing up the horse and wagon they began to pack. The hardest thing was them telling their kids, grand kids, and great grandkids that they were leaving and not planning on returning.

To explore why the trip was necessary. Lorain's family was really close, she had a sister and brother in Chicago, two brothers within 60 miles of their old home, and one that perished in the Denver bombing. She never even got the chance to call them or say goodbye. She got up and fled with her husband when the shit hit the fan. Those open wounds would not let her leave this world peacefully. Blake, being the loving husband and never believing he was too old for anything, suggested one final trip south. If they perished on the trip, they would do it together. Traveling from the great north would not be easy. They could go east and catch a pirated fishing vessel south on the lake or just trudge directly south over land. They eventually decided the overland route would be the best.

Now the wagon they would be pulling was an interesting piece of technology. It was an old military diesel MRZR-D4-AF UTV built for the deserts of the middle east. According to the manual, the -AF (All Fuel) version was never supposed to see the private sector. Its fuel technology was still considered top secret. Blake had only used it one other time for a scouting mission. Their first destination would be an old Walmart some 150 miles south of the compound. The last time they were there was 15 years prior. It was in a now lifeless, desolate area that was hit by a massive resurge of some COVID like infection that killed everyone and everything. Since it had been 15 years ago, the risk was worth it for some diesel super fuel. The military UTV was designed to run on anything that burns, like the old Humvee's from the 1980's. The diesel super fuel was simple, every burnable additive from the automotive section and every bottle of vegetable oil or motor oil that had not gelled, from any large store, would be mixed to a thin oily consistency. Since Blake had fashioned an overhead tank and filtering system on the top of the massive desert attack vehicle, he figured it had a range of about 1000 miles between refueling stops. The collecting, mixing, testing, and loading would be the hardest task for the older couple.

Blake had come up with this idea years before when he found the oversized, overly expensive UTV in the garage of one of those, super-rich vacation assholes, which used to come to the area. The amount of money they would spend on the most unique UTV to outdo the other guy was crazy. When Blake first found it and had read the mill spec manual for it, he was impressed. He took a gallon of turkey frying oil and a bottle of lighter fluid and made himself his first batch of fuel. It would run on pure oil, but the manual recommended thinning it down with any other petroleum product. His biggest confusion was, if military vehicles can run on just about anything but water, why did his old truck only run on high-priced gasoline. The damn government sure new how to stick it to people back then.

With the "Wagon" loaded and hitched to the two large horses they had captured a few years back; they were ready to start the trek south. Rudy and Zed, the two new leaders of their compound, did not want to see them go off on this fool's errand, but knowing their parents, there was no telling them no. So, the long trip down old state road 45 started. The weeds were high, and the forest had mostly taken everything back, but it was still passable. Not many old dead cars or trucks would be found this far north. They would have to deal with that in about a week once they got close to the wild west of the Madison enclave. The massive crater down in Bob's crossing was a sight to see. The makeshift bomb that Bernie set off really did some damage.

The trek towards the COVID-zone was quiet. Blake and Lorain talked about the old-days when they would just go for a drive in Blake's big Bronco, that he spent way too much money on. They reminisced about a time that didn't exist anymore, and to most alive today, had never existed. Once they were close to the old monolithic structures of the old Walmart, Menards, and some old grocery store, they got a bit anxious. Pulling up inside an old strip mall, Lorain noticed an old auto-parts store sitting off in the corner. Pointing to it, she asks Blake if that wouldn't have everything they need without risking going into the superstores. Blake, being hardheaded and not thinking about the small details, could not believe he had missed it. "Of course, that will be way easier and the weeds and old cars in the lot will keep us completely hidden", he thought to himself.

After scouring the old auto parts store and getting more than enough oil and additives together, Blake and Lorain began mixing their first batch in an old empty oil recycling barrel. Luckily this barrel was new and had not been used yet, the others sitting around had thick black gelatinous gunk filling them. Once Blake got the thickness he wanted, he went and cleaned the shelves of his secret ingredient. Sea Foam was an old time additive invented back in the 1980's. This stuff never went bad. Adding a 10 to 100 ratio to the super fuel should be all it needs. Filling the priming tank first and winding the old boat crank, a spring-loaded starter he had built years ago, he turned on the ignition and let it spin. Nothing on the first try, nothing on the second, but the third try rewarded him with the old multi-fuel diesel firing to life. The cool thing about these special military engines is they needed zero electricity to run. Sure, they had a power system to run the equipment after they started, but it was not a necessity. They set the horses free and rolled out with the UTV under its own power.

The trip started out boring, the first 100 miles were completely desolate. No human presence at all. Once the couple got within 50 miles of the Madison enclave, that changed. Now you can remember those old movies where the entire village lives outside the castle; this was that on steroids. The diesel motor of their UTV was very quiet as far as combustion motors went, but the sound of it must have traveled for miles. It was not the only self-propelled vehicle, but definitely the most unique. Blake pulled his scarf over his face and Lorain did the same. He said in a low voice, "Keep your face covered, at our age, we will look like easy targets." Lorain, being Lorain, pulled her short barrel AR15 from her bag and leaned it on the top of the door rail. No one was going to mess with her. Heading more west than south, the couple tooled along at about 20 miles per hour. Whenever an obstacle was encountered, it was Blake's job to get around it and Lorain's job to keep them secure. Only once did she have to fire off a small burst of fire to scare a large group from pushing an old car in front of them. Having ammunition for these guns was as rare as having them at all.

Heading away from the enclave toward Iowa was now the plan for getting farther south. They could travel about 700 miles before needing to blend up some more fuel. Heading towards Waterloo Iowa, the two figured they could blend and refuel somewhere around there. The farmland was one of two ways. Fully farmed as known in the past, or extremely overgrown. These farmed sections were smaller but looked fully farmed and maintained. The piles of old, discarded, equipment were no longer visible at every farm. This equipment was now the new technology everyone wanted. They did see a few old tractors pulling some of this old equipment, but the mega combines and eight wheeled tractors sat as the new, old and discarded equipment.

Traveling south through Iowa, with the tank reaching 50%, Blake and Lorain began to look for a way to refuel their vehicle. About an hour later, a stream of about 10 ATVs came flying out of the woods. These things were really moving, and everyone was armed. Now, armed is relative, but 10 double barreled shotguns pointed at you can really mess up your day. The leader of the group, who introduced himself as Farmer John, pulled up next to Blake and simply said howdy. Blake pulled his scarf down and asked his wife to do the same. They kind of figured that hiding their age was not going to help.

John, being a man of about 50 years of age, smiled and said, "Damn grandpa, what the hell are you doing on this beast traveling through my county?" Blake just smiled, and replied, "We are headed over to my wife's family stomping grounds in Illinois. We want to see if anyone is still there, or are they long gone?" Johns' eyes dropped to the ground, and he said, "Mine are gone, killed by punks, just me and my merry band of brothers farm this entire valley. We are mostly peaceful around here, so we are not going to stop you, but we do ask that you continue outside of our area.

And watch out for the crazies around the Illinois border. We hear some of them actually eat people."

Blake smiled and said, "We will just keep moving, but we would like somewhere we could refuel. Once we are in Illinois, I have a feeling we will need to get out quickly and will not have time to do it." John, being curious, ask, "What does this crazy machine run on?" Blake tried to explain that the thing would run on anything that burns. "A simple set of valves allows me to go from diesel type fuels, which we are currently running on, to gas, alcohol, propane, natural gas, and even hydrogen; if it burns, this thing can run on it." John just smiled and said, "If you have anything to trade, I can give you more alcohol than you can carry." Blake popped out of his seat and walked to the rear where several large ammo type boxes were mounted and hit the lock release. Handing a box to John, he simply said, "This is what I call my force equalizing box system. I will trade one of these for your fuel." John popped it open, and his eyes went wide. He quickly closed the box, smiled and said, "Sir, you have a deal."

After hoisting a 55-gallon barrel onto the last empty section of the roof, Blake shook John's hand and said goodbye. Looking like he was losing a friend, John exclaimed, "If you survive this, stop by on your way home. We don't meet many decent people anymore. You are both welcome here." Heading out towards their next destination, Lorain asked, "What was in that ammo can?" Blake smiled and responded; "Do you remember traveling in that military vehicle that Tom gave us? It was full of 5.56 ammo and those three rifles. In the bottom of each of those extra-large ammo boxes, I put 500 rounds of that ammo and one of those AR15 pistols we took from that gun shop in Wisconsin. I figured they would make the ultimate trading packages."

They rambled into the town of Sterling Illinois some 22 hours later, battered, and tired. Blake and Lorain were exhausted. They traveled to the small cemetery where Lorain's family has been interned for the past 100 years. The couple set up a small perimeter security system and pitched their tent. They would not find any living relatives here, but it was their first official stop in Illinois. Close enough to their destination but still far enough away from major population centers. The fallout from the nuclear blasts in Chicago hopefully would be still far enough away to not make them sick.

After a day of reminiscing around the headstones of her father and others, it was time to plan the next leg of their journey. Two main destinations were considered. The small town where her mother lived and passed away 20 years ago, and their old house where Ben had passed as they rescued their grandchildren. The conversation got a bit tense from time to time but they eventually decided that their original homestead was their next destination. After all, Blake had lived there for 55 years and knew every road and path in the area. Even though the house would be a pile of ashes, the location was as secure as an area around there could be. The creek, the woods, and the general area was formerly their home.

The trip southeast was quiet and eerie. The blasts from Chicago cleaned out the area more than expected. No fuel would be found along the way, but that was okay. They had a total of about 900 miles worth of their super-fuel diesel and the alcohol from farmer John. The plan was to get to the Illinois river and then follow it south. Eventually they would find one of the bridges still standing and not taken over by thugs, they hoped. Once they saw the dreaded I80 in the distance feelings of joy and fear arose. Interstates were not somewhere you wanted to be. Plugged with dead cars, they became the super refugee camps that ran for hundreds of miles. Maybe now, 20 years later they were abandoned. At least that is what they hoped.

Cruising under an old overpass, they quickly got as far away from the interstate as they could. Just the staying awake and bouncing around in the buggy was ready to kill the older couple, but they kept going. Heading southeast trying to avoid any large cities, they traveled through desolate overgrown areas. When the river finally appeared and the old Henry bridge stood tall, unbroken, and unmanned, they were ecstatic. They waited until night and then cruised as slowly and quietly up one side of the bridge as they could. Once at the top, a loud crack hit the role bar just below the fuel tank. Blake screamed; "Hold on, we are taking fire." Blake hammered the throttle and the UTV launched. This thing was designed to outrun anything out in the desert, so when you wanted this thing to go, it would go. It was probably less of a UTV and more of a desert dune buggy. Hitting the other side at about 85 miles per hour, the UTV was just a blur. Reaching the old route 26 was quick and dangerous. This place had more run ins between cars and deer than anywhere else in the state. Blake quickly picked an old driveway and headed up the hill flooring it all the way. It was a gamble, but a lot of these places were abandoned before the collapse, some of them had to still be standing.

Lying prone on the floor of an abandoned house, Blake searched his scope for any light source. It was so dark out, no one could find them, he hoped. Lorain was already asleep. That woman had learned to sleep anywhere. She did this like an old action star from some ridiculous old movie. "Sleep when you need it and then get back to work" was her motto. The morning came and the couple decided to lay low for at least three days before they moved. They had a hand pump well behind the house that actually worked and enough wild edibles to eat like royalty. Not to mention the hundreds of squirrels everywhere.

The two sat and talked about what the hell they were doing. They were not going to find anyone. The last people in the area they knew were Ben and Amber. Ben died in their arms and Amber was never seen again. She was presumed dead on the back side of the property where the final attack came from. So, why are they even here, were they just bored? The question fell silent and was not brought up again. They decided to hit the old homestead tomorrow. They would lay some flowers where their son and daughter-in-law perished and then head home.

Running along the river for 30 more miles and then up through the hills for maybe ten would bring them close. They saw people in some places, but most feared the vehicle and ran for cover. No one under 20 was going to be used to them. They tooled through what was once the rich people's area up on a huge hill. Then down into the valley again. They passed burned out houses of people they knew. Everything looked like an apocalypse movie, it was unreal.

Not a half mile from their destination, an arrow came flying from somewhere and damn near skewered Blake. He cranked the wheel and headed for a half burned out house that was a friend of his years back. The UTV crashed through the wall and landed in what looked like Big Al's bedroom. With all the humor he could muster, Blake said, "I am getting too old for this shit." Lorain just looked at him, she eventually responded, "I am tired, if they are going to kill us, at least we will go together. But I really don't want to be skewered, and spit roasted for dinner". With that note, the large box behind them was opened. Body armor, rifles, and every sort of tactical gear from yesteryear came out. Looking like a couple of geriatric soldiers, the two headed for the street. Screaming like a madman, Blake yelled, "This is my fucking neighborhood, my son died here, my friends died here, and if you get in our way, you will die here also. We lived at 301 Clearview Street. That is where we are going. Just let us pay our respects and then we will leave."

The Stormms' stiffened as a strange howl was heard, it seemed like there were hundreds of them. A half dozen fully camouflaged people came running from the woods. Lorain fired off short bursts at the ground in front of them and screamed, "Back the hell up, dying here is not what you want today." A short stocky person appeared from the woods next to an old park. A female voice rang out; "That house is a pile of ashes. My husband was killed at that house, my children disappeared at that house, and I was left for dead in those woods. This is my fucking neighborhood." Drawing back a compound bow, the woman launched an arrow towards the two. Blake threw himself to the ground as the arrow just narrowly missed his head. Lorain fired off another burst and screamed, "If you hurt my husband, I will kill every last one of you." Blake screamed again, "How could your husband of died in that house, I burned it to the ground after my son died there. That was my house, and no one will stop me from getting to it." A silence fell over the area. Lorain lowered her weapon and walked across the road; she stared the woman in the face, and said in a low voice. "Amber?"

Sitting around a large fire, on a large plot of land with another burned out house in the front, Amber, Blake, and Lorain told their stories. The older couple told how they rescued John and Rachel when Ben was killed. How they took them north and they were living on their land with two of their uncles. They both have found significant others from a settlement they trade with 150 miles to the east. The first settlers to come back to that area since the Russian invasion. They even let Amber know she was now a grandma. Amber told of their old neighbor, Tom, finding her and nursing her back to health. He helped organize what was left of the survivors before he fell sick to cancer and died five years ago. His buddies now made up their security forces and trained the younger ones to survive. Amber picked up and handed Blake an old, battered compound bow. "Dad, this is the one you gave me 25 years ago. It has saved countless lives; it has been my only friend since Ben died. I want to see my babies, please take me home."

Big Al's House: Rolling up on his old house, a nearly dead, 80-year-old, Big Al was bewildered. He had decided a few years back to come home to where his mom was buried, and his friends had lived to put a close on his life. His house was burnt, and it looked like someone had driven through it. Sitting on his latest vehicle that he scavenged, a large draft horse, he just stared. He climbed down and hobbled to the old front door. Digging around in his pocket, he pulled out his old key and placed it into the lock. To his surprise, it still turned. Inside his house, everything was burned and destroyed. Al sat down on what was a chair some 20 years before and closed his eyes. Drifting off to sleep, Big Al would never wake up again. He was home.

In the weeks ahead the three reunited survivors along with a dog, and two orphaned young girls traveled north. The UTV was too small for the group to use, so it was traded to a neighboring town for an old 1980's Humvee H1 in near perfect shape. The owner had meticulously restored it before the collapse. It was found in his underground garage along with a dozen other exotic vehicles. Pulling a matching military trailer, the trip began. Blake's idea for making his super fuel worked as well in the lumbering beast as it did in the UTV. He only had to worry about the fuel filters on it. Luckily, the guy who restored it retrofitted the filter system with the most common farm tractor fuel filters in the world. Every farm store in the country had 10 plus of these on their shelves. Breaking down, hopefully, would not be an issue. The Stormm's were just to worn out for it.

The group traveled back through Iowa to see Farmer John on the way. They exchanged stories and Blake gave John one more of the cool, force-equalizing boxes that he had. They stayed farther away from the Madison enclave this time to keep safe. They went a bit too far north and almost got killed by the Minneapolis North Central Militia. A group of city gang bangers that ruled that area. Calling themselves a militia was almost a joke.

Three weeks later, a tattered old couple and three survivors rolled onto the property. Blake, nearly getting shot by his own sons slowly got out with his hands in the air trying to let them know it was them. Rachel, with her rifle shouldered, closed in on the Humvee and demanded the rest of the occupants get out. "Everyone, hit the dirt!" she screamed. When Amber and Rachel's eyes met, an awkward silence arose. Neither really recognized each other, they just stared. As Rachel's finger tightened around the trigger, the silence was broken by John, who had come in with flex cuffs to secure the occupants. "Mom!"--"Is that you?"

Chapter 18 – The History

The history of the world after the collapse was a bit clouded. The information that the Stormms' gathered came from ham radios, strangers, and surprisingly enough, an old AM talk radio network out of Canada that started transmitting about 15 years after the collapse. They compiled what history they could into their compounds journal. It is as follows: The grid went down on July 9th, twenty 25. All technology-based services were hit simultaneously by an AI super virus or a Polymorphic Self-replicating Algorithm to be more technical. The virus was sponsored by the Peoples World Liberation Group. The group was a North Korean, Saudi Arabian and Russian consortium set on taking down capitalism. They had it written and implemented by a rouge faction of a Silicon Valley tech think-tank company called "Power to The Planet." They most likely did not think it would spread like it did. But being a polymorphic virus meant it could rewrite or change itself as it needed, and it did. The general concept was a small bit of code, which could run on devices as slow as the oldest cellular phones, was spread to every internet connected device on the planet. It would act like a parasite operating system, which made it hard to detect or remove. It remained hidden for about nine months before it was triggered. It had simple instructions, propagate itself, find weakness and exploit. This is where the creators really screwed up. The polymorphic code did not understand what it was asked to do by exploit, so it made up what it was supposed to do over a billion times.

Since every infection acted like its own spoiled child, there was no way to chase them all down.

Grid racing was one of the most destructive payloads it came up with. From what they could piece together, it involved ramping the voltage up and down across the grid at a high rate until literally everything connected had a massive failure. Think about it like this, lightning strikes an object, then you quickly ground it out. Seconds later it strikes again, and you do the same. Do this a thousand times over the course of five minutes. The result cascaded in its destruction. When traffic lights failed accidents happened, completely gridlocking every major city. When infrastructure control systems failed, power plants, dams, natural gas pumping stations, and other services most people never heard of, all failed.

The second real catastrophe was the damn Russians trying to take advantage of the chaos and launching a 3-pronged attack. Since the Russian nuclear arsenal was still 100% air gapped from the world, it was so easy for them to launch 13 ICBMs at the already burning USA. The target map was not understood until the land invasion started. Atlanta, DC, Chicago, New York, and Denver were the only large cities bombed. The other eight were targeted at strategic fault lines and tectonic plate intersections. When the new Madrid fault in the Northern Kentucky and Southern Illinois area was hit, the entire area was destroyed in a 9.7 earthquake. A massive canyon formed from the fault all the way up to Carbondale. Supposedly the bombs were going to give them a path to connect from Canada down to Florida to cut the country in half. Most People had heard about what happened to them in the north. When the Russians sent three divisions across the Sault Ste Marie International Bridge; a massive bombing campaign with every still functioning plane and bomb started. Somewhere around Rosedale Michigan, what was left of the US military, dropped so many bunker buster bombs on and around the invaders that the Great North US Sink Hole was formed. Being over 100 miles across and immediately filled with water from Lake Nicolet, all the invading forces were literally washed away. Later becoming the latest addition to the Great Lakes, known as Sink Hole Lake. Some speculate that the New Madrid fault earthquake opened a deep under the crust fisher that formed the hole. And it was only triggered by the bombing run.

The United States Military fractured and split. The Army National Guard, run by General Rages Jones, went completely rogue. They re-branded themselves as the ANG. They oppressed and murdered their way from Canada down to Texas. Dedicated Marines, regular Army and the Air Force were in constant battle with the rogue group. Groups like the Stormms' took major tolls on the ANG from coast to coast.

The Florida invasion did not make it outside of that state. Nobody knows why the Russians did not keep driving north from there. That area is now known as the Russian Cuban American Province. No news ever comes from there. It is said that the mine field separating it from the rest of the continent is ten times larger than the old North and South Korean border mine field.

California was damn-near dropped into the ocean. Three of the largest nuclear bombs ever built were dropped along the San Andreas Faultline. These were not air burst like the others; they were ground burst in the lowest possible place. One of them was shot directly down into an old mineshaft. That one was so effective, the crust split all the way up into Oregon and over to Idaho. The earthquake it caused was so massive, it topped out the Richter scale.

The country of New Texas was not a surprise to anyone. Texas had been threatening to secede from the US for over 100 years. The Texas National Guard was assumed by the Texas State Guard one day after the collapse. They closed all the state boarders and invaded Mexico two weeks later. They had also taken over part of Louisiana, Mississippi, and Alabama, which gave them complete control of the gulf all the way to Florida. Texas had enough isolated power stations to where they remained about 60% powered. They were not going to share with anyone in the former USA. Note: Blake's sister lived in central Texas. He always wondered if she survived. Last bit of rumor heard was that the New Texan Army was heading towards Panama. With all their conquered lands, they would end up being about a quarter the size of what was left of the former US.

The rest of the old US 48 lower states is divided up and run like an old feudal system. Some areas have 20th century style power stations up and running, but it does not amount to much. If you are fortunate enough to get connected, you are restricted to 10 amps of service for about four hours a day. The general count of loss of life for the former USA was around 73%. That left less than nine million left alive and most of them were the rural, self-sufficient type. Few large cities even existed as much more than toxic wastelands. The East Coast was decimated by the sheer number of large cities and people living there. Those people had zero survival skills and had mostly perished within the first month after the collapse. Cannibalistic tribes of the worst mankind could create were moving from town to town, consuming everything and everyone. Like a plague of locusts, they moved. Driven by sheer insanity and hunger. The rest of the world might have fared better or worse than the USA did, but no one would know.

Survivors banded together in enclaves, towns, and modern-day fortresses. Groups in the north fared better than groups in the south or on either coast. Northern groups were mostly left alone but still faced challenges, factious dictators and just flat-out crazy people were most of their worries. The country of Canada just ceased to exist. What was left banded together under a new flag and called themselves the "Northern Wilderness Survivors." They would end up going to war with England over what they called, "The Territory of the King."

Epilogue.

The seasons came and the seasons went. The Stormm's families and friends grew with every day. Children would become parents; grandchildren would find love and the Stormms' would find piece.

After years of use, Blake's old school Ham radio had finally died, and the compound could no longer receive the bouncing signals from long distances. Information now came on foot from the people wanting a new life in the far north. The attacks came less and less; the good people came more and more. The area around to Stormm's was teaming with new life and hope.

As the matriarch of the Stormm's world took her last breath while holding Blake's fragile wrinkled hand, he looked around the compound. It had grown into its own small town. It was no longer just the original four or five people. He looked up at his two surviving sons and said, "Lorain has passed, I will not be far behind her. Take us to the first grove of trees we planted. Place us there." As his sons protested, Blake kissed his wife ever so gently and closed his eyes one last time. He drifted off this plane of existence, towards his next adventure.

Standing under the massive walnut tree, the people of Stormm Town paid their last respects. Not many of them really knew the Stormms' but they knew what they did. When the killing stopped; the Stormm's invited all of them to stay, they only needed to pull their own weight, and they would be protected.

As the procession passed and flowers were laid on the freshly dug soil, Zed opened the box labeled, final wishes. He had no idea what was in it. A small piece of paper titled "Our Song" with some lyrics on it was inside. Zed cleared his throat and began to sing.

"If I sit here
If I just sit here
Would you sit with me and just ignore the world?"

The Stormm's story was a saga of survival, loss, and love. Their family and friends lived and died through the entire collapse. In the silence left by the grid's fall, some had found not just a way to survive, but to thrive. Their extended family stood as a beacon of hope, a testament to the enduring strength of the human spirit and the unbreakable bonds of family.